Intermediate

READING

READING POWER

111學年度起學科能力測驗、全民英檢中級適用

跨閱英文

Read Across Boundaries

附翻譯與解析

編著者
王信雲
學歷：國立交通大學英語教學所碩士
經歷：桃園市立壽山高級中學英語科教師

審定者
車畇庭
學歷：美國賓州印第安那大學語言學博士
經歷：國立政治大學外文中心副教授

三民書局

序

知識，就是希望；
閱讀，就是力量。

在這個資訊爆炸的時代，應該如何選擇真正有用的資訊來吸收？
在考場如戰場的競爭壓力之下，應該如何儲備實力，漂亮地面對挑戰？
身為地球村的一分子，應該如何增進英語實力，與世界接軌？

學習英文的目的，就是要讓自己在這個資訊爆炸的時代之中，突破語言的藩籬，站在吸收新知的制高點之上，以閱讀獲得力量，以知識創造希望！

針對在英文閱讀中可能面對的挑戰，我們費心規劃 Reading Power 系列叢書，希望在學習英語的路上助你一臂之力，讓你輕鬆閱讀、快樂學習。

誠摯希望在學習英語的路上，這套 Reading Power 系列叢書將伴隨你找到閱讀的力量，發揮知識的光芒！

推薦序

　　《跨閱英文》是一本以「跨」作為理念所出發的書，其中包括「跨文化」、「跨世代」以及「跨領域」三個面向。為什麼以「跨」為規劃的出發點呢？因為生活在現代的我們，每天所面臨的社會就是一個充滿「跨」的環境。不同語言文化背景的人們天天穿梭在我們周遭的大街小巷中，主流文化和各種次文化共存於我們的社區中，不同世代的價值觀不斷地激發出各種火花以及討論，斜槓人生更是幾乎每個人都朗朗上口的一個詞彙或越來越普及的社會現象。

　　每天都在「跨」來「跨」去的我們，怎麼能不多了解一點這些就發生在我們身邊的議題呢？新課綱中所重視的素養，語言是溝通的工具，批判性思考、跨文化溝通的敏銳性等都在這本書中有了最好的體現！從簡短且程度適中的文章中，我們探討了「跨文化」、「跨世代」以及「跨領域」三個面向的各種議題，希望讀者能夠在豐富又有趣的選文中，回頭思考自己的理解與判斷，並能夠更客觀地去評斷各種現象與議題。

　　我一直相信，議題的討論或批判性思考的訓練，不是只能在閱讀長篇大論或艱深的文章後才能進行。因此，心裡一直希望能規劃出一本內容相對簡單，但具有深度及討論價值的閱讀書。我非常榮幸與開心自己有機會參與這一本書的規畫，也特別希望利用這個機會感謝多年前一起合作 *HEAD START I* 和 *HEAD START II* 的 Schafer 李德能 (李悅) 老師，因為這兩本書是《跨閱英文》最初的雛形。當然，更開心有機會和理念相同的王信雲老師一起合作！

　　最後，希望每天「跨」來「跨」去的我們，都能夠因為這一本書而在不同文化、不同世代以及不同領域中優游自在的「跨」起來！

三民 / 東大英文教材主編

車昀庭

2

給讀者
的話

　　部頒課綱中所強調之「核心素養」，指一個人為適應現在生活及迎向未來挑戰，所應具備的知識、能力與態度。換句話說，核心素養強調學習不宜以學科知識及技能為限，應結合不同的生活情境，培養解決問題的能力並實踐所學。

　　《跨閱英文》一書可作為普羅學習者培養英文中短文閱讀能力的營養補充劑。素養閱讀練習貴在「精」，而不在囫圇吞棗。對於無法在日常生活中大量閱讀的忙碌學習者來說，《跨閱英文》中含「跨文化」、「跨世代」、「跨領域」為特色之閱讀素材，文長約 180 至 400 字的跨領域及跨學科選文，內容平易近人，更包含新課綱中所強調的情境化閱讀配方。對於在新課綱下忙於開設各式多元課程的教師來說，《跨閱英文》也可以成為難得的新素養導向試題來源，具多元且有層次的評量設計，新增同時包含選擇題與非選擇題的混合題型，再配合其後的「進階練習」、「字彙實力」和「延伸練習」，循序漸進的實戰演練，更能協助忙碌的教師輕鬆差異化教學，培養學生訊息處理的邏輯思考（如：分析、整合）技能，進而因應未來生活與學習所需。

　　衷心期許《跨閱英文》能協助學習者掌握跨學科基本知識，也培養在不同情境中判斷、整合與表達的能力，更盼望本書能提供第一線教學夥伴更多的資源和靈感，使英文素養閱讀及試題更俯拾即是、平易近人！

劉信雲

目次 Contents

Part 1

 跨文化

Part 2

跨世代

Part 3

跨領域

Photo Credits

All pictures in this publication are authorized for use by: Shutterstock.

使用說明

STEP1 混合題型

符合 111 學年度起學科能力測驗的最新題型，先閱讀左頁文章，理解該文章內容後回答右頁混合題，包含標號題、圖片選擇題、表格填充題等。

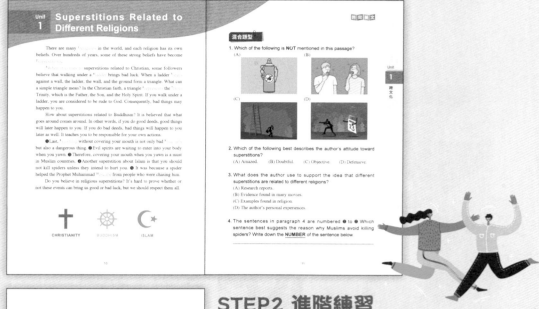

STEP2 進階練習

結合各式圖片、圖表和表格題，達到整合知識和活用英文的能力。

STEP3 字彙實力

附詞性和中譯，每課精心彙整 10 個實用字彙，豐富字彙寶庫。

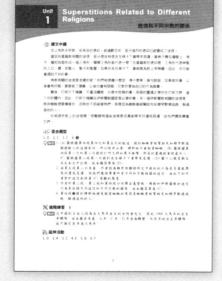

STEP4 延伸活動

涵蓋多元的趣味性活動，可作為課堂活動，也可在自學中培養學習英文的樂趣，讓你 *FUN* 學英文。

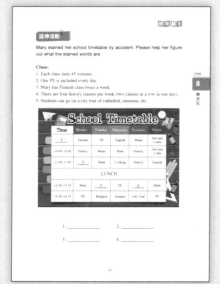

STEP5 解析夾冊

隨書附活動式解析本，包含中譯和解析，方便作答後檢視。

The outline of any culture may be a different picture in the eyes of different people.

—*Jacob Burckhardt*

跨文化

Cross Cultures

任何一個文化的輪廓，在不同人的眼裡可能是一幅不同的圖畫。

——雅各·布克哈特

Unit 1 Superstitions Related to Different Religions

There are many [1]religions in the world, and each religion has its own beliefs. Over hundreds of years, some of these strong beliefs have become [2]superstitions.

[3]When it comes to superstitions related to Christian, some followers believe that walking under a [4]ladder brings bad luck. When a ladder [5]leans against a wall, the ladder, the wall, and the ground form a triangle. What can a simple triangle mean? In the Christian faith, a triangle [6]represents the [7]Holy Trinity, which is the Father, the Son, and the Holy Spirit. If you walk under a ladder, you are considered to be rude to God. Consequently, bad things may happen to you.

How about superstitions related to Buddhism? It is believed that what goes around comes around. In other words, if you do good deeds, good things will later happen to you. If you do bad deeds, bad things will happen to you later as well. It teaches you to be responsible for your own actions.

❶Last, [8]yawning without covering your mouth is not only bad [9]manners but also a dangerous thing. ❷Evil spirits are waiting to enter into your body when you yawn. ❸Therefore, covering your mouth when you yawn is a must in Muslim countries. ❹Another superstition about Islam is that you should not kill spiders unless they intend to hurt you. ❺ It was because a spider helped the Prophet Muhammad [10]escape from people who were chasing him.

Do you believe in religious superstitions? It's hard to prove whether or not these events can bring us good or bad luck, but we should respect them all.

CHRISTIANITY   BUDDHISM   ISLAM

混合題型

1. Which of the following is **NOT** mentioned in this passage?

(A)

(B)

(C)

(D)

Unit

1

跨
文
化

2. Which of the following best describes the author's attitude toward superstitions?

(A) Amazed.　　(B) Doubtful.　　(C) Objective.　　(D) Defensive.

3. What does the author use to support the idea that different superstitions are related to different religions?

(A) Research reports.

(B) Evidence found in many movies.

(C) Examples found in religion.

(D) The author's personal experiences.

4. The sentences in paragraph 4 are numbered ❶ to ❺. Which sentence best suggests the reason why Muslims avoid killing spiders? Write down the **NUMBER** of the sentence below.

_____

Astrology may also cause superstitions. For example, the Japanese used to believe that girls born in 1966, the year of Fire Horse, would become "fire horse women." They are considered to be risks to their future husbands. Such a superstition influenced the birth rate. The birth rate dropped sharply in 1966.

According to the passage, which of the following is most likely the year of Fire Horse?

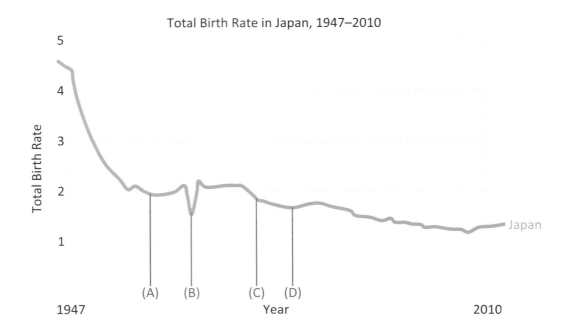

Total Birth Rate in Japan, 1947–2010

❶ religion (n.) 宗教

❻ represent (v.) 代表

❷ superstition (n.) 迷信

❼ holy (adj.) 神聖的

❸ when it comes to (phr.) 當談到

❽ yawn (v.) 打呵欠

❹ ladder (n.) 梯子

❾ manners (n.) 禮貌

❺ lean (v.) 靠在

❿ escape (v.) 逃跑

延伸活動

Read the passage given below. Fill in the blanks by choosing the most appropriate words (A–F) from the given options.

(A) religion	(B) leaning	(C) triangle
(D) superstition	(E) ladder	(F) falling

Do you know walking under a ladder might bring you bad luck? There are many reasons for such a ___1___. One of the explanations has its roots in ___2___: the Holy Trinity—the Father, the Son, and the Holy Spirit—is in the shape of a sacred ___3___. Therefore, walking under a leaning ladder would break the Trinity.

Besides, most people don't walk under a ___4___ because it is just unsafe. If a ladder is ___5___ against a wall and someone is standing on it, you definitely don't want to face the risk of something ___6___ on your head.

Whether you believe in this superstition or not, we had better understand the meaning behind it and not go through under a ladder.

1. _____   2. _____   3. _____   4. _____   5. _____   6. _____

Harvest Celebrations in Different Names

The [1]harvest celebration is to [2]count your blessings, and thank for everything. In the United States, it is called "Thanksgiving Day." The Amis [3]tribes in Taiwan celebrate "Harvest Festival." In Germany, it is named "Erntedankfest." In Korea, they call it "Chuseok." In Western Africa, such as Ghana and Nigeria, "Yam Festival" is used to refer to their harvest celebrations.

Regardless of the different names, food plays a major role in the harvest celebrations. A good harvest means enough food on the table for everyone. So, people would express their [4]gratitude to God or their [5]ancestors for their [6]assistance in bringing in the harvest. At the same time, people enjoy and share food with the family and [7]relatives. The ways people celebrate their festivals are various. It can include singing, dancing, parading, or even setting off fireworks. The traditional songs and dances are [8]essential to Amis Harvest Festival. In Germany, people [9]praise and worship God in the churches during this time. In some countries, such as the United States, Thanksgiving Day lasts for only one day. But Chuseok lasts for a few days in Korea.

Although [10]customs may **vary** according to different cultures, the idea of giving thanks on this special day is the same across the world.

混合題型

1. What is the passage mainly about?

   (A) The food people usually have on national holidays.

   (B) The ways people show their gratitude to their relatives.

   (C) The dates of the harvest celebrations in different countries.

   (D) The traditions of the harvest celebrations around the world.

2. Below is a poster. According to the passage, which of the following organizations would most likely hold this activity?

   (A) Korea Tourism Organization.

   (B) West Africa Tourism Organization.

   (C) German Academic Exchange Service.

   (D) Digital Museum of Taiwan Indigenous Peoples.

3. Which is closest in meaning to the word "**vary**" in the last paragraph?
   (A) Grow.　　　(B) Differ.　　　(C) Disappear.　　　(D) Exchange.

4. Fill in the blanks with the information contained in the passage about how people call their harvest celebrations.

	how people call their harvest celebrations
the United States	Thanksgiving Day
the Amis tribes	_____
Germany	Erntedankfest
Korea	_____
Ghana	Yam Festival
Nigeria	_____

The following chart shows the average cost of Thanksgiving dinner.

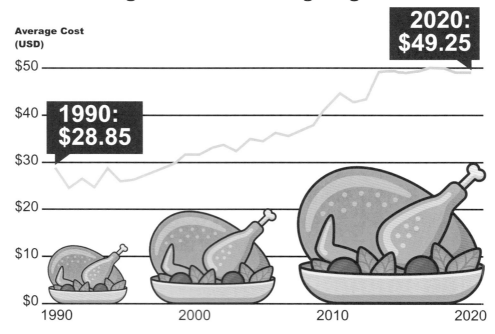

Average Cost of Thanksgiving Dinner

According to the chart, which of the following statements is true?

(A) People spent the least money on Thanksgiving dinner in 2000.

(B) People paid less for Thanksgiving dinner in 2020 than in 2010.

(C) The cost of Thanksgiving dinner in 1990 is lower than the one in 2020.

(D) The cost of Thanksgiving dinner has decreased over the past thirty years.

字彙實力

❶ harvest (n.) 收成

❷ count your blessings (phr.) 知足

❸ tribe (n.) 部落

❹ gratitude (n.) 感謝

❺ ancestor (n.) 祖先

❻ assistance (n.) 幫助

❼ relative (n.) 親戚

❽ essential (adj.) 必要的

❾ praise (v.) 讚頌

❿ custom (n.) 習俗

延伸活動

The following is a recipe for roast turkey. Match the pictures (A–E) to the correct steps.

Steps:

_____ 1. Preheat an oven to 175°C.

_____ 2. Season the turkey with the herb mixture.

_____ 3. Stuff the turkey with chopped orange, onion, and carrot.

_____ 4. Bake the turkey in the preheated oven until it turns golden brown.

_____ 5. Remove the turkey from the oven, and be ready to slice it.

Unit

2

跨
文
化

(A)

(B)

(C)

(D)

(E)

Unit 3 Washing Powder and Political Correctness

"Ancient Chinese Secret" is a TV [1]commercial from the 1970s. Do you know what this commercial is for? Is it for a book about medicine or a recipe? In fact, it is a commercial for [2]washing powder!

❶ You might be [3]wondering if Chinese people are famous for washing clothes. ❷ Of course not! ❸ However, in the early days, many Chinese immigrants made a living by doing the laundry in the United States. ❹ That is why, Americans usually think of Chinese people when it comes to washing powder. ❺ That sounds a bit [4]ridiculous, right?

[5]As a matter of fact, many commercials contain [6]stereotypes of a certain race or gender. These commercials may be humorous to some of the audience, but they can be [7]offensive and even [8]insulting to others. For example, when people saw a black man's face and his super white teeth on the cover of the product named Darkie, they probably would guess that it is toothpaste. However, the political and social trends suggest that people value racial and sexual equality. Since the 1980s, advertisers have increasingly used [9]politically correct language in the commercials. Afterward, Chinese people have stopped selling any ancient secret of washing powder in the commercials, and Darlie **has taken over from** Darkie. Even so, some advertisers are still promoting their products in a stereotypical way. It is common to see a woman doing the laundry in the commercials which promote the washing machine, especially on Mother's Day. When it comes to car commercials, you usually see a man driving a car, not a woman.

[10]All in all, next time if you happen to see commercials in the media, you can pay attention to any possible stereotypes hidden behind them. You might be surprised to see what you have found.

1. What is the purpose of this passage?

   (A) To encourage freedom of speech.

   (B) To reveal some stereotypes in the mass media.

   (C) To explain why Chinese immigrants sell washing powder.

   (D) To show racial discrimination in the working environment.

Unit

3

跨
文
化

2. The sentences in paragraph 2 are numbered ❶ to ❺. Which sentence best suggests the reason why washing powder is associated with Chinese people? Write down the **NUMBER** of the sentence below.

_____

3. Which is closest in meaning to the phrase "**has taken over from**" in the third paragraph?

   (A) Has put.

   (B) Has replaced.

   (C) Has broken.

   (D) Has repeated.

4. Which of the following can be inferred from this passage?

   (A) Today's advertising is easy to understand.

   (B) Stereotypes cannot be seen on the products anymore.

   (C) Not only Americans but also Africans that know the ancient secret.

   (D) Discrimination still can be seen in some commercials.

Which of the following best illustrates sexual equality?

(A)

(B)

(C)

(D)

字彙實力

❶ commercial (n.) 商業廣告

❷ washing powder (n.) 洗衣粉

❸ wonder (v.) 疑惑

❹ ridiculous (adj.) 可笑的

❺ as a matter of fact (phr.) 事實上

❻ stereotype (n.) 刻板印象

❼ offensive (adj.) 冒犯的

❽ insulting (adj.) 侮辱的

❾ politically correct (adj.) 政治正確的

❿ all in all (phr.) 總而言之

延伸活動

"When it comes to . . ." is used to introduce or identify one specific topic that is being talked about. Complete the following sentences with the given words creatively.

1.

When it comes to my talent,

_____ .

2.

When it comes to traffic,

_____ .

3.

When it comes to traveling,

_____ .

4.

When it comes to New York,

_____ .

Unit 4 The Culture of Food

Food gives us an important **window** on the world. Different parts of the world have very different food cultures. Food varies from region to region. Have you ever wondered why people eat a particular type of food?

In today's world, berries that grow in Chile can be flown to Germany quickly [1]owing to the efficient means of [2]transportation. **Fresh seafood can be prepared in Japan and shipped to one of the chain restaurants in Taipei in just a few hours.** However, it is not always this way. In the past, people lived on the food that was [3]available in the place they lived. In other words, the environment made a strong [4]impact on their food choices.

❶Hakka people in Taiwan, for example, ate Hakka foods to [5]stand up to their difficult living conditions in the early days. ❷ Most of Hakka people used to do lots of [6]physical work, and therefore they preferred a more [7]intense flavor. ❸Additionally, they needed to transport goods over mountains for many days. ❹ To preserve the food for a longer time, the Hakka were expert in dried, salted, or [8]pickled foods. ❺ However, people in Peru have eaten mainly potatoes for centuries. ❻ These underground vegetables are easily grown here and help people to survive in the cold and dry climate. ❼Over the years, they have grown over 3,000 [9]varieties of potatoes. ❽Nowadays, Peru is one of the biggest exporters of them.

Our choice of food is influenced by not only what we like but also what we can get from the environment. From the discovery of different foods in different areas, people can find that each food culture is so [10]unique.

Potatoes in Peru

22

1. How does the author begin the passage?

(A) By giving a question.

(B) By mentioning an incident.

(C) By providing statistics.

(D) By comparing people's responses.

2. What does "**window**" refer to in the first paragraph?

(A) An opportunity to do something.

(B) A way of learning about something.

(C) A box appearing on a computer screen.

(D) An opening covered by a sheet of glass.

3. What is the purpose of the sentence "**Fresh seafood can be prepared in Japan and shipped to one of the chain restaurants in Taipei in just a few hours.**" in the second paragraph?

(A) To indicate that Taiwanese prefer Japanese food.

(B) To explain how Japan exports seafood to other countries.

(C) To prove that transportation really changes our diet.

(D) To emphasize the importance of international trade.

4. The sentences in paragraph 3 are numbered ❶ to ❽. Which sentence best explains the reason why people in Peru eat potatoes? Write down the **NUMBER** of the sentence below.

_____

Which of the following best illustrates the main idea of this passage?

(A)

(B)

(C)

(D)

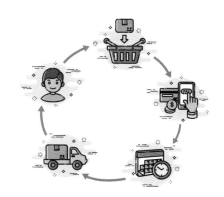

字彙實力

❶ owing to (phr.) 由於

❻ physical (adj.) 身體的

❷ transportation (n.) 交通工具

❼ intense (adj.) 濃烈的

❸ available (adj.) 可獲得的

❽ pickled (adj.) 醃製的

❹ impact (n.) 影響

❾ variety (n.) 不同種類

❺ stand up to (phr.) 承受得住

❿ unique (adj.) 獨特的

延伸活動

Fill in the blanks with the options given below. Discuss different foods with your partners and match each country to its national dish.

(A) the United States	(B) France	(C) Germany	(D) Japan	(E) India
(F) Mexico	(G) Spain	(H) Italy	(I) England	(J) Greece

1. _____

TACO

2. _____

FISH AND CHIPS

3. _____

PAELLA

4. _____

PIZZA

5. _____

GREEK SALAD

6. _____

PRETZEL

7. _____

SUSHI

8. _____

CHEESEBURGER

9. _____

CROISSANT

10. _____

CURRY

Unit 5 When in Rome, Do as the Romans Do

When you go ¹sightseeing or make a business trip around the world, you'd better know local customs. Otherwise, there might be some ²misunderstandings. For example, when things are going well, people put their thumbs up in the United States and in Taiwan. However, if you do this in Australia, the Middle East, and some countries of West Africa, you are ³insulting others. In Taiwan, if someone makes a circle with their thumb and forefinger, it means "OK." ⁴On the contrary, it is insulting to Brazilians and Greeks.

The meaning of the same ⁵gesture can vary differently throughout the world. Therefore, it is important to figure out what the gestures mean in the country you are visiting. It could help you not to get into trouble. If you ⁶attempt to make a good ⁷impression when meeting people for the first time, you have to know how to greet them. When you are in Japan, you ⁸bow to people. In Western countries, shaking hands and kissing both cheeks are ⁹generally acceptable.

❶How about the eating habits? ❷In East Asia, people eat with chopsticks while knives and forks are used in the West. ❸In India, people only use their right hands to pick up food. ❹They mix their food together, roll it into little balls, and put them in their mouths with their fingers. ❺The left hands, however, shouldn't be used while dining because Indian people often use it in the bathroom. ❻Therefore, eating with the left hands is a definite no-no in India.

¹⁰As the old saying goes, "When in Rome, do as the Romans do." That saying may help you much more than you think.

In East Asia

In the West

In India

1. How does the author begin the passage?

   (A) By providing statistics.

   (B) By mentioning an incident.

   (C) By giving some examples.

   (D) By comparing people's responses.

2. According to the passage, which of the following is a picture that shows how the Japanese greet people for the first time?

   (A)   (B)   (C)   (D)

3. The sentences in paragraph 3 are numbered ❶ to ❻. Which sentence best indicates the reason why the Indians don't pick up food with their left hands? Write down the **NUMBER** of the sentence below.

   _____

4. Where does this passage most likely appear?

   (A)   (B)   (C)   (D)

      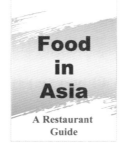      

Look at the following situations. Why are people's responses to Mary and John's gestures so different? Which of the following best explains the reason?

Situation A

Mary and John's Gestures	People's Responses

Situation B

Mary and John's Gestures	People's Responses

(A) Gestures are clear to understand.

(B) The same gestures have different meanings.

(C) Different gestures lead to different eating habits.

(D) Mary and John make rude gestures at people in situation A.

字彙實力

❶ **sightseeing** (n.) 觀光

❷ **misunderstanding** (n.) 誤解

❸ **insult** (v.) 侮辱

❹ **on the contrary** (phr.) 與此相反

❺ **gesture** (n.) 手勢

❻ **attempt** (v.) 試圖

❼ **impression** (n.) 印象

❽ **bow** (v.) 鞠躬

❾ **generally** (adv.) 通常地

❿ **as the old saying goes** (phr.) 俗話說

延伸活動

According to the passaqe, fill in the blanks with the options given below. Match the customs to the correct countries.

(A)	(B)	(C)	(D)	(E)
the Middle East	Taiwan	Europe	Brazil	India

Customs:

_____ 1. Putting a thumb up means insulting people.

_____ 2. Making a circle with a thumb and a forefinger means insulting people.

_____ 3. Eating with chopsticks.

_____ 4. Eating only with the right hand.

_____ 5. Eating with a knife and a fork.

Unit

5

跨
文
化

Unit 6 Cosplay

❶ Have you ever seen Pikachu, Spider-Man, or other anime [1]characters walking on the street? ❷ If you have, they might be cosplayers. ❸ Cosplay is a mix of "[2]costume" and "play." ❹ It began as the act of dressing up as characters from anime, manga, video games, [3]science fiction movies, etc.

In the 1980s, cosplay firstly got the attention of Japanese anime fans. These fans gathered round, shared ideas, and acted like their favorite characters. As the number of cosplayers increased, more cosplay festivals were held. A wave of cosplay then [4]swept Asian countries and the West in the 1990s. Nowadays, cosplay festivals in different countries are held annually and attract thousands of fans.

Some cosplayers are interested in designing and creating beautiful and interesting costumes. Others focus on acting. These cosplayers study their chosen characters and try to "become" them. As a result, there are many [5]contests being held. They are for the best costume, the best cosplayer, and so on. Moreover, people are having fun dressing up as the characters of both the same and [6]opposite sex.

Many people who see cosplayers for the first time may consider them a little silly, strange, or simply [7]childish. However, it is [8]evident that cosplay is an enjoyable [9]hobby. It gives people a platform to use their [10]imagination and have fun. So, if you want to cosplay, which character would you choose to be?

1. What is this passage mainly about?

   (A) The advantages of being a cosplayer.

   (B) The description of cosplay and cosplayer.

   (C) The cultural background of Japanese anime.

   (D) Guidelines for cosplayers about cosplay festivals.

2. Which newspaper column does this passage most likely appear in?

   (A) The travel column.

   (B) The sports column.

   (C) The culture column.

   (D) The financial column.

3. The sentences in paragraph 1 are numbered ❶ to ❹. Which sentence best indicates where the characters that cosplayers dress up as from? Write down the **NUMBER** of the sentence below.

   _____

4. Which of the following can be inferred from the third paragraph?

   (A) Cosplayers only focus on costume.

   (B) Good costumes always cost a fortune.

   (C) A man can be dressed as a female character.

   (D) To win the contests, people need to be professional actors.

Which of the following best illustrates the second paragraph?

(A)

Gender of the Cosplayers

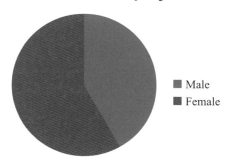

■ Male
■ Female

(B)

Ages of Cosplayers

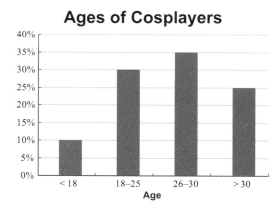

(C)

Average Costume Size Chart

(cm)	S	M	L
Chest	90	95	100
Waist	70	75	80
Hip	95	100	105
Height	160	165	170

(D)

字彙實力

❶ **character** (n.) 人物，角色

❷ **costume** (n.) 服裝

❸ **science fiction** (n.) 科幻 (電影)

❹ **sweep** (v.) 風行

❺ **contest** (n.) 比賽

❻ **opposite** (adj.) 相反的

❼ **childish** (adj.) 幼稚的

❽ **evident** (adj.) 顯而易見的

❾ **hobby** (n.) 嗜好

❿ **imagination** (n.) 想像力

Each across and down word has a clue. Look at the following clues, solve the puzzle, and write down the words (which are mentioned in the passage). Some of them have been done for you.

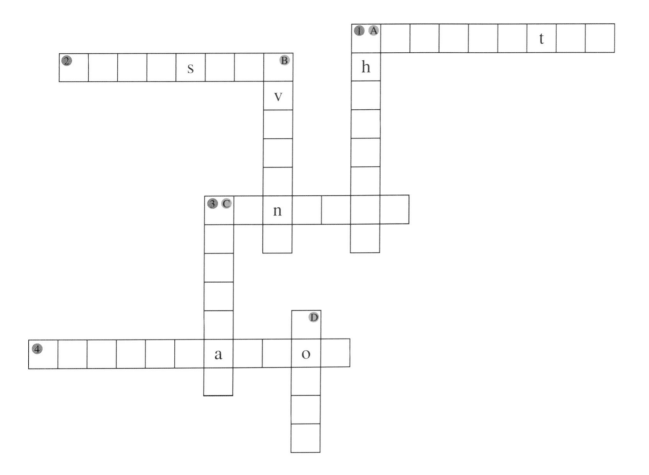

Clues:

Across	**Down**
① A role in a movie or play.	Ⓐ Behaving like a child.
② Completely different.	Ⓑ Clear and obvious.
③ Competition.	Ⓒ The act of dressing up as a character.
④ The pictures that you create in your mind.	Ⓓ An activity that you do for fun.

❶ I haven't slept well in the last three months. ❷ I sleep only for a few hours at night and wake up in the early morning. ❸ The reason for my ¹sleepless nights is my daughter, Lara. ❹ New babies ²rarely sleep through the night. ❺ Since Lara was born three months ago, I have been waking up several times every night.

Are you wondering where my wife is during my nights with Lara? My wife is asleep. She has to go to work the next day. In Norway, over the years, parents receive ³more and more paid ⁴parental leave. A particular leave is ⁵reserved for fathers, and it cannot be transferred from fathers to mothers. Parents then ⁶divide the rest of the parental leave period.

Laws and regulations on parental leave differ among countries. Before the child turns three, both the mother and the father can ⁷apply for a maximum of two years of parental leave in Taiwan. Moreover, they can receive a monthly ⁸allowance of 60 percent of their monthly ⁹salaries for the first six months. However, in the United States, most of the labor is not entitled to parental leave.

I have friends who still believe that it is a mother's job to stay home and raise a child. However, I think that both parents should take the responsibility and get to know the new baby. I wouldn't ¹⁰trade my sleepless nights with Lara for anything.

1. The sentences in paragraph 1 are numbered ❶ to ❺. Which sentence best indicates Lara's age? Write down the **NUMBER** of the sentence below.

_____

2. What is the third paragraph mainly about?
   (A) A confession of failure.
   (B) A proof of a father's guilt.
   (C) A statement on the policy change.
   (D) A description of parental leave in different countries.

3. Which of the following countries' laws and regulations on parental leave is **NOT** mentioned?
   (A) The United States.
   (B) Taiwan.
   (C) Sweden.
   (D) Norway.

4. Which of the following can be inferred from this passage?
   (A) The author feels pleased to take parental leave.
   (B) His friend is willing to take parental leave.
   (C) His wife is busy taking care of a child at home.
   (D) In Norway, each of the parents takes short paid parental leave.

The following chart illustrates the length of paid parental leave in four countries. Which of the following can be inferred from the chart?

Paid Parental Leave

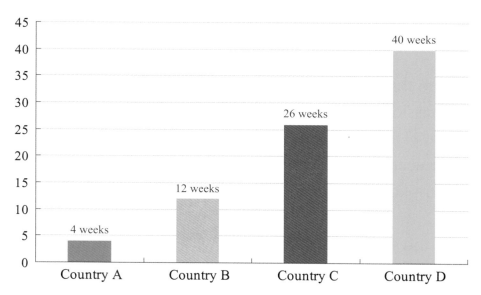

(A) No one can take paid parental leave in country D.

(B) In country C, people can take 26 weeks of paid parental leave.

(C) Among country A, B, C, and D, people in country A take the longest paid parental leave.

(D) People in Country B can get more pay than those in country C.

字彙實力

❶ **sleepless (adj.)** 失眠的

❻ **divide (v.)** 分配

❷ **rarely (adv.)** 很少

❼ **apply (v.)** 申請

❸ **more and more (phr.)** 越來越多

❽ **allowance (n.)** 津貼

❹ **parental leave (n.)** 育嬰假

❾ **salary (n.)** 薪水

❺ **reserve (v.)** 保留

❿ **trade (v.)** 互相交換

延伸活動

It's sb's (n.) to (v.)

An example in the passage:

It is a mother's job to stay home and raise a child.

Make sentences by putting the given words in the right order.

1. (a firefighter's mission / It's / the fire out / to put)

_____.

2. (his or her seat belt / every passenger's responsibility / It's / to fasten)

_____.

3. (It's / the household chores / to do / each family member's duty)

_____.

Less Is More

It ¹comes as no surprise that most parents are ²concerned about their children's education. As a result, this concern often ³translates into "more"— more classes, more exams, more homework, and more ⁴pressure on children.

❶ People in Finland, however, ⁵adopt a different ⁶approach—the "less is more" ⁷philosophy. ❷ ⁸Generally speaking, Finnish students spend less time having formal education and more time acquiring other types of knowledge. ❸ In Finland, students also spend less actual time in school. ❹ A ⁹typical school day starts at 9 a.m. and finishes at around 2 p.m. ❺ This gives students more time to relax and develop their own interests. ❻ Furthermore, teachers can have more time to prepare lessons and support students who need extra assistance. ❼ It is also not surprising that there are fewer exams in Finland since they believe that ¹⁰academic performance is not everything. ❽ Although students have fewer exams and less homework, they are still educated well, and even excel in their studies.

Does this approach work? The results have been amazingly good. According to many studies, Finland has some of the top students in the world as well as some of the happiest ones. So, it seems clear that when it comes to education, perhaps less is actually more.

1. Which of the following is the best slogan for this passage?

(A) No pains, no gains.

(B) Dream big and dare to fail.

(C) Another practice of learning.

(D) Higher education promises success in life.

2. Which of the following best describes the author's attitude toward the "less is more" philosophy?

(A) Doubtful.

(B) Positive.

(C) Negative.

(D) Sarcastic.

3. According to the passage, which of the following is true?

(A) Students in Finland attend school for eight hours a day.

(B) Teachers in Finland don't have to prepare lessons.

(C) The Finnish approach to education may be worth learning.

(D) Having less free time and more exams is the key to a good education.

4. The sentences in paragraph 2 are numbered ❶ to ❽. Which sentence best suggests the reason why there are fewer exams in Finland? Write down the **NUMBER** of the sentence below.

_____

Which of the following best illustrates the "less is more" philosophy mentioned in this passage?

(A)

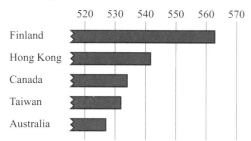

Average Score on Science Test Scale

(B)

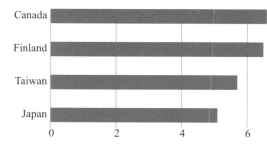

Education Spending (% of GDP)

(C)

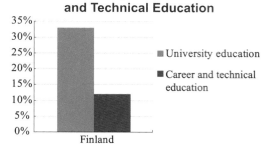

Percentage of People in Finland Who Have a University Education or Career and Technical Education

(D)

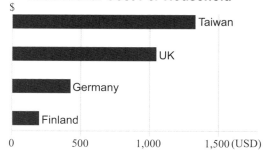

Educational Cost Per Household

字彙實力

❶ **come as no surprise (phr.)** 在預料之中

❻ **approach (n.)** 方法

❷ **concerned (adj.)** 擔憂的

❼ **philosophy (n.)** 哲學

❸ **translate (v.)** 轉變

❽ **generally speaking (phr.)** 一般來說

❹ **pressure (n.)** 壓力

❾ **typical (adj.)** 典型的

❺ **adopt (v.)** 採取

❿ **academic (adj.)** 學業的，學術的

延伸活動

Mary stained her school timetable by accident. Please help her figure out what the stained words are.

Clues:

1. Each class lasts 45 minutes.
2. One PE is included every day.
3. Mary has Finnish class twice a week.
4. There are four history classes per week (two classes in a row in one day).
5. Students can go on a city tour of cathedral, museum, etc.

School Timetable

Time	Monday	Tuesday	Wednesday	Thursday	Friday
1	Finnish	PE	English	Music	Arts and Crafts
10:00–10:45	History	Music	Math	History	Arts and Crafts
11:00–11:45	2	Math	Cooking	History	English
LUNCH					
12:30–13:15	Math	3	PE	4	Math
13:30–14:15	PE	Religion	Science	City Tour	PE

1. _____   2. _____

3. _____   4. _____

Life is like riding a bicycle. To keep your balance, you must keep moving.

—*Albert Einstein*

跨世代
Cross Generations

人生就像騎腳踏車。想要維持平衡，你必須持續前進。

——阿爾伯特・愛因斯坦

Looking for Love

Love and marriage then and now are so different. In the past, the decision about a future husband or wife was often made by their families. Young people were expected to marry young. A man and a woman were usually not permitted to be alone together until they were married. When they met, a chaperone would follow. The chaperone was usually an elderly lady, and her job was to make sure that the young people would ¹behave themselves. So, the young couple could only ²chat with each other, and kissing or holding hands were not permitted. The rule about dating behavior was quite strict at the time.

³By comparison, our society today is different. People often marry late or live independently. The influence of family is not so powerful on single people. Most of them in their thirties are ⁴too independent to be controlled by their parents. However, some of them still ⁵seek the opinions among their families and friends. They are arranged to go on a ⁶blind date.

❶ Nowadays, more and more people use technology to assist them in search of true love. ❷ ⁷Online dating is becoming more popular. ❸ People use online dating websites and online dating apps on smartphones to find their partners. ❹ They first build up a ⁸profile and display their best qualities. ❺ With these efficient methods, they can find more ⁹suitable ¹⁰candidates to go out on a date with. ❻ However, only time will tell if these methods can result in lasting relationships.

Past   Present

混合題型

1. How is this passage organized?

(A) In the sequence of time.

(B) In order of importance.

(C) By cause and effect.

(D) In order of frequency.

2. What is the passage mainly about?

(A) The advance in the way people date.

(B) The challenges for young singles.

(C) The limitations of late marriage.

(D) The influence a chaperone brought.

3. According to the passage, which of the following is true about a chaperone?

(A) A chaperone treats young people to dinner.

(B) A chaperone plays with young unmarried people.

(C) A chaperone is usually an old lady.

(D) A chaperone would allow young people to drink.

4. The sentences in paragraph 3 are numbered ❶ to ❻. Which sentence best indicates the author's attitude toward the effect of online dating websites and dating apps? Write down the **NUMBER** of the sentence below.

_____

Unit

9

跨
世
代

Below is a passage from a post on social media.

"I am Kelly, 26 years old. I am outgoing and cheerful. Besides, I am a cat person. Moreover, I am a shop owner selling quality products. I am looking for someone who is creative and has many new ideas. We must have a lot to talk about."

Look at the picture below. Who stands a better chance of being Kelly's future partner discussed in the passage?

_____

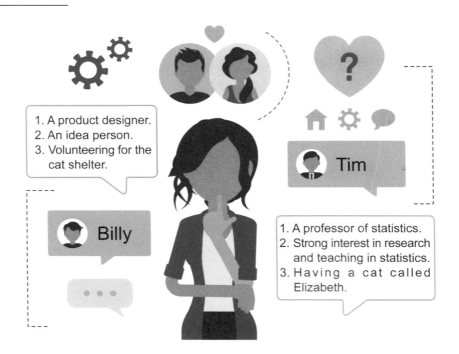

1. A product designer.
2. An idea person.
3. Volunteering for the cat shelter.

Billy

Tim

1. A professor of statistics.
2. Strong interest in research and teaching in statistics.
3. Having a cat called Elizabeth.

字彙實力

❶ **behave (v.)** 表現得體

❷ **chat (v.)** 聊天

❸ **by comparison (phr.)** 相比之下

❹ **too . . . to . . . (phr.)** 太⋯以致於不⋯

❺ **seek (v.)** 尋找

❻ **blind date (n.)** 相親

❼ **online dating (n.)** 線上約會

❽ **profile (n.)** 簡介

❾ **suitable (adj.)** 合適的

❿ **candidate (n.)** 候選人

延伸活動

現在進行式 "am / are / is + V-ing" 用法之一，表示「越來越」之意，動詞多用 go / get / turn / become 等。

Look at the following pictures. Make sentences by putting the given words in the right order.

1. (dating / more / Online / popular / is becoming)

_____.

2. (are / My / becoming / old / parents)

_____.

3. (in the / are turning / red / The leaves / park)

_____.

The Greatest Inventions of All Time

Our world is shaped by many brilliant ¹inventions. Light ²bulbs allow us to easily work and have a social life at night. Modern forms of transportation, such as cars, trains, and airplanes, allow us to travel great distances fast. Printing ³presses allow information to be ⁴spread widely among many people. Electronics, such as radio and television, allow us to receive and pass on information globally. New technologies, such as the Internet and smartphones, allow us to communicate with people immediately all over the world. **What inventions are the most important to you and what could you live without?**

Imagine a world without some of these wonderful inventions. Without cars or other efficient means of transportation, we would have to live very close to our office. If our family lived far away, we would only be able to visit them maybe once every few years. Travel would be a luxury we could not ⁵afford. We would not have a chance of exploring the world and learning about different cultures. Without printing presses, information would not be spread rapidly. Without the Internet or even telephones, communication would be difficult because letters might take weeks to be ⁶delivered. Our understanding of the world would be limited. Our worldview would be poor.

Humans have created lots of successful inventions. Over the ⁷generations, great inventions have changed our way of living and our way of looking at the world. Without some of these amazing inventions, we would all be less ⁸informed, less ⁹connected, and more ¹⁰isolated. We should learn from the past and look to the future. What new inventions do you think we need to bring a better future?

In the Past   Now

混合題型

1. How is the information about the inventions organized in this passage?

   (A) In order of importance.　　(B) In order of frequency.

   (C) By comparison and contrast.　　(D) By classification.

2. What is the purpose of the sentence "**What inventions are the most important to you and what could you live without?**" in the first paragraph?

   (A) To provide the main idea of the first paragraph.

   (B) To express the author's personal opinion.

   (C) To arouse readers' interest.

   (D) To persuade readers to agree with the writer.

3. If you want to look for the answers to the question in the last paragraph on the Internet, which of the following keywords would most likely be used?

   (A) Inventions needed in a better future.

   (B) A brief history of the Internet.

   (C) The best inventors of all time.

   (D) The inventions in our daily life.

4. Fill in the blanks with the information contained in the passage about these wonderful inventions.

	advantage(s)
light bulbs	allow us to easily work and have a _____ at night
airplanes	allow us to travel great distances fast
television	allow us to _____ on information globally
smartphones	allow us to _____ people immediately all over the world

Unit

10

跨
世
代

49

Where does this passage most likely appear?

(A)

(B)

(C)

(D)

字彙實力

❶ invention (n.) 發明

❷ bulb (n.) 電燈泡

❸ press (n.) 印刷機

❹ spread (v.) 散布

❺ afford (v.) 負擔

❻ deliver (v.) 遞送

❼ generation (n.) 世代

❽ informed (adj.) 見多識廣的

❾ connected (adj.) 有聯繫的

❿ isolated (adj.) 孤立的

延伸活動

From question 2 to 10, please put the letters in the right order to form a word. (These words are mentioned in the passage.) The first word has been done for you. Then, put the letters highlighted in yellow in the right order for the eleventh word.

1. lbub   b | u | l | b

2. acr

3. atnir

4. pilreaan

5. rpgitnin

6. ridao

7. liinevteso

8. elnehpote

9. tIrnente

10. eohrpastnm

11.

Unit 11 Blue for Boys, Pink for Girls?

We can find out the sex of a baby months before it is born. Some parents even throw gender [1]reveal parties. Friends and family are all gathered round a special cake. Then, they cut a piece out and the secret is revealed—blue cake [2]layer for a boy and pink for a girl. However, what does it really mean to be a boy or a girl? More and more people are starting to question the need to [3]identify a [4]specific gender at all.

Traditionally, boys have been praised for their [5]strength. Whether they are on the soccer field or at home with a group of friends, boys are thought to have plenty of energy. Girls, on the other hand, are expected to [6]be willing to talk about their feelings with one another. They may interact with other people in an [7]emotional way rather than in a calm one. From a very young age, boys are taught that it is not okay to cry, **while** it is fine for girls to cry.

❶These gender stereotypes are doing more harm than good. ❷Whether you identify qualities as [8]hardness or softness, all humans have a mix of everything in them. ❸The reality is that a little boy can love to play soccer and also spend time making dumplings in the kitchen. ❹A little girl can enjoy playing with dolls and also love [9]solving math problems. ❺Only when society stops putting pressure on people to behave in certain ways will people enjoy [10]genuine pleasure of being themselves.

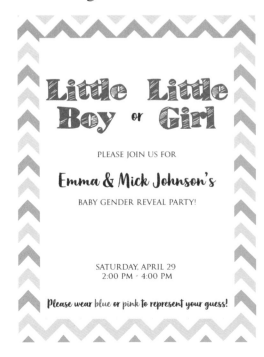

Little Little
Boy or Girl

PLEASE JOIN US FOR

Emma & Mick Johnson's

BABY GENDER REVEAL PARTY!

SATURDAY, APRIL 29
2:00 PM - 4:00 PM

Please wear blue or pink to represent your guess!

1. On which of the following websites would this passage most likely be found?

> 🔍 gender   🎤

(A) An Introduction to Gender and Climate Change | Global Climate Daily
https://www.globalclimatedaily.com
Do you know the connection between gender and climate change ...

(B) Gender Equality | Gender Equality Club
https://www.genderequalityclub.com
Focus on equality between males and females. Until now, gender equality is still one of the biggest social issues of our time ...

(C) Gender Similarities in Biology | Sex Education News
https://www.sexeducationnews.com
What are the similarities between men and women in biology? Let's find out more about gender similarities in biology ...

(D) Useful Guide to Planning a Gender Reveal Party | ABC Diaper
https://www.abcdiaper.com
Here are some useful tips on how to throw a great gender reveal party, including the theme, food, decoration, and so forth.

Unit

11

跨
世
代

2. Look at the page of the online dictionary. Which of the following is the meaning of the word "**while**" in the second paragraph?

(A) during the time that
The doorbell rang while Susan was in the kitchen.

(B) although
While Mary was tired, she kept working.

(C) and in contrast
I am single while my sister is married.

(D) a period of time
It took me a while to finish my homework.

3. The sentences in paragraph 3 are numbered ❶ to ❺. Which sentence best indicates the solution to the problem of gender stereotypes? Write down the **NUMBER** of the sentence below.

_____

4. According to the passage, which of the following is true about gender?

(A) It is the only factor that forms our habits.

(B) It is not decided until the gender reveal party.

(C) Gender is the rule that decides what boys and girls should do.

(D) It is not a way to judge one's personality.

進階練習

Which of the following best illustrates the main idea of this passage?

(A)

(B)

(C)

(D)

字彙實力

❶ reveal (v.) 揭露

❷ layer (n.) 層

❸ identify (v.) 辨認

❹ specific (adj.) 明確的

❺ strength (n.) 力量

❻ be willing to (phr.) 願意

❼ emotional (adj.) 情緒性的

❽ hardness (n.) 剛

❾ solve (v.) 解答

❿ genuine (adj.) 真的

延伸活動

Draw a path through ALL the letters to form a word that matches the clue. The first one has been done for you.

1. Clue: fairness

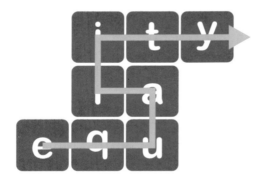

2. Clue: particular

3. Clue: recognize

4. Clue: power

Unit 12 Is SOHO Suitable for You?

Do you want to stay at home and make money? Do you like to wear whatever you like when you work? Do you enjoy ¹flexible working hours? Are you okay with an irregular ²income? Do you hate to have a boss? If you say "yes" to all these questions, you are a good SOHO candidate, which ³stands for people working in a small office or home office.

❶ ⁴Thanks to the rapid growth of ⁵digital technology, almost anyone can ⁶make a living by being a SOHO worker! ❷Some of the popular choices are being a ⁷freelancer, Internet ⁸celebrity, website designer, or online seller. ❸Imagine how wonderful it would be if you can make money without leaving home and work without a boss around! ❹It must be a dream job for many people.

While SOHO workers enjoy many advantages that regular workers don't, being a SOHO worker is actually not as good as it seems. First of all, you may not have any income for months! Secondly, you need to come up with new ideas, services, or products all the time in order to make a profit. ⁹On top of that, you have to work harder than anyone else in a regular office for lack of support and resources a company may provide. Last, because your boss is not around, you need to be very ¹⁰diligent in your work and organize yourself to meet all the deadlines.

Being a SOHO worker can be a lot of fun. However, whether you can be successful or not depends on your personality and self-discipline. So, are you ready to be a SOHO worker?

SOHO Worker

VS

Office Worker

1. What is this passage mainly about?

(A) The history of working time.

(B) The method of starting a SOHO business.

(C) A possible mode for working.

(D) A new digital technology for SOHO workers.

2. The sentences in paragraph 2 are numbered ❶ to ❹. Which sentence best suggests the reason why people are able to work at home? Write down the **NUMBER** of the sentence below.

_____

3. Which is closest in meaning to the word "**On top of**" in the third paragraph?

(A) Besides.   (B) Except for.

(C) At the peak of.   (D) On the edge of.

4. According to the passage, which of the following is most likely a SOHO worker?

(A) Sam Smith.   (B) Jill Wagner.   (C) Mary James.   (D) Bobby Brown.

Unit

12

跨
世
代

The following chart shows the percentage of people with different educational levels that work at home.

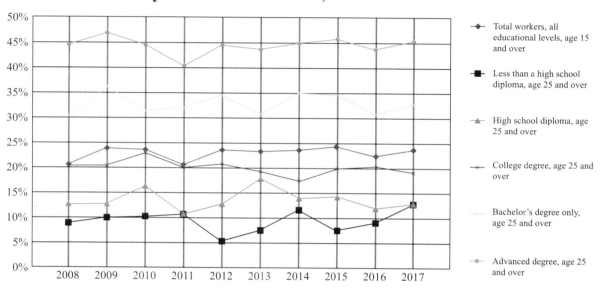

Percentage of people being SOHO workers, by educational levels, 2008–2017

According to the chart, which of the following statements is true?

(A) There was a sharp rise in the number of people working at home in 2011.

(B) The percentage of workers working at home in 2017 is the lowest.

(C) For those aged 25 and above, the higher education they have, the more likely they choose to work at home.

(D) Those with a high school diploma always enjoy more privilege of SOHO businesses than those with higher educational levels.

字彙實力

❶ flexible (adj.) 彈性的

❷ income (n.) 收入

❸ stand for (phr.) 代表

❹ thanks to (phr.) 由於

❺ digital (adj.) 數位的

❻ make a living (phr.) 謀生

❼ freelancer (n.) 自由業者

❽ celebrity (n.) 名人

❾ on top of (phr.) 除⋯之外

❿ diligent (adj.) 勤勞的

延伸活動

Based on the clues, place the following characteristics (A–J) into the correct blank.

(A) determined	(B) greedy	(C) honest	(D) jealous	(E) patient
(F) quiet	(G) responsible	(H) selfish	(I) talkative	(J) violent

Characteristics	Clues
1. _____	I don't talk much.
2. _____	I always tell the truth.
3. _____	I always want more than I need.
4. _____	I always think of my own advantage.
5. _____	I have a duty to take care of this project.
6. _____	I tend to use physical force to hurt someone.
7. _____	I feel angry and unhappy when someone has something that I want.
8. _____	I can deal with lots of routine work without getting upset.
9. _____	I don't allow anyone or anything to stop what I am going to do.
10. _____	I tend to talk a lot or enjoy having a talk with people.

Unit

12

跨
世
代

LGBTQIA Pride, from New York to Taipei

On the last Saturday in October, many people ¹parade through Taipei, cheering and waving rainbow flags. This is a typical scene of Taiwan LGBTQIA (lesbian, gay, bisexual, transgender, queer, intersex, and asexual) Pride Parade, which started in 2003 and has been held annually ²since then. The first event was not so big that only around two thousand people were at the parade. However, over the years, more people, regardless of their genders, are willing to ³take to the streets to support the ⁴campaign.

❶It all started one night in 1969 in New York. ❷That night, the police arrived at a gay bar called *The Stonewall Inn* and began to arrest people without reasonable cause. ❸ People at the bar were angry at the police and big fights ⁵broke out. ❹ Later, the bar was ⁶surrounded by many angry members of the lesbian and gay community. ❺ The police were forced to hide inside the bar for their own safety. ❻ The struggles had been going on for several days before they ended. ❼ In the following year, the first gay pride parade was held to remember this important event. ❽The fights around *The Stonewall Inn* ⁷inspired many people to stop accepting any bad treatment from the government and to be brave to ⁸stand up for their rights instead.

Later on, a great variety of LGBTQIA pride ⁹marches began to be held annually in many big cities across the world, such as New York, Helsinki, and Birmingham. So far, many countries, including Taiwan, have ¹⁰legalized same-sex marriage. LGBTQIA rights are gradually emphasized and respected around the world.

混合題型

1. Which of the following best illustrates LGBTQIA Pride mentioned in this passage?

   (A)

   (B)

   (C)

   (D)

2. Which of the following can be inferred from this passage?

   (A) The first pride parade was held before the Stonewall event.

   (B) The number of participants in the parade has been decreasing yearly.

   (C) People celebrate their pride marches in many big cities worldwide.

   (D) Pride parade in Taiwan has been held every two years since 2003.

3. Which of the following is the best slogan for this passage?

   (A) Breaking the glass ceiling.

   (B) Love has no gender.

   (C) Always listen to your mom.

   (D) Save the bottle. Save the planet.

4. The sentences in paragraph 2 are numbered ❶ to ❽. Which sentence indicates why the first gay pride parade was held in 1970? Write down the **NUMBER** of the sentence below.

   _____

"LGBTQIA" stands for "lesbian, gay, bisexual, transgender, queer, intersex, and asexual." Which of the following is created in this way?
(A) "BBQ" stands for "barbecue."
(B) "Blog" stands for "weblog."
(C) "Brunch" stands for "breakfast and lunch."
(D) "BBC" stands for "British Broadcasting Corporation."

字彙實力

❶ **parade (v.)** 遊行

❷ **since then (phr.)** 此後

❸ **take to the streets (phr.)** 走上街頭

❹ **campaign (n.)** 活動

❺ **break out (phr.)** 爆發

❻ **surround (v.)** 包圍

❼ **inspire (v.)** 激勵

❽ **stand up for (phr.)** 維護

❾ **march (n.)** 示威遊行

❿ **legalize (v.)** 合法化

延伸活動

Read the passage given below. Fill in the blanks by choosing the most appropriate words from the given options.

(A) campaign	(B) inspire	(C) struggles	(D) equal	(E) stand up for

Holding LGBTQIA pride marches is important. The purpose of our annual LGBTQIA __1__ is to call the public's attention and to make the society more inclusive. Through parades, we take to the streets and encourage individuals to support the view that everyone is __2__, including LGBTQIA people.

We want to __3__ people to embrace who they are and respect everyone's differences. It remains true that challenges and __4__ certainly drive us to grow and go forward. We are determined to __5__ our rights.

Unit

13

跨世代

1. _____   2. _____   3. _____   4. _____   5. _____

Unit 14 Travelers in Different Times

What is your idea of a perfect vacation? For some people, a pleasant trip may be spending a week on a beautiful beach. Others may enjoy staying in a ¹luxury hotel at the end of the week. For many young people, the best kind of travel may be a ²journey to every corner of the world on their own.

In the past, many people booked trips through ³travel agencies and followed the tour guide. This way of traveling is called a "package tour." They paid the travel agencies for the details, such as transportation, and everything will be all ⁴settled. However, starting in the 1960s, young travelers decided to do things differently. They got rid of the heavy baggage and tour guides. In addition, they made ⁵arrangements all on their own and traveled with as few items as possible.

❶ These travelers became known as backpackers who traveled with backpacks. ❷ They used public transportation, stayed in youth ⁶hostels, and ate local food. ❸ Their goal was to see the world and spend only little money. ❹ They wanted to travel for a longer period of time to learn more about themselves and the countries they visited.

Over the years that followed, backpackers traveled around the world. Some ⁷hitchhiked, some biked, and some even walked from place to place. Today, young people's traveling style has ⁸evolved from backpacking into ⁹couch surfing. Instead of staying in hotels or youth hostels, travelers sleep on the couches at local people's houses. They believe that this is the best way to experience local culture and ¹⁰explore the world.

Travel Agency

Follow a Tour Guide

Backpackers

Hitchhikers

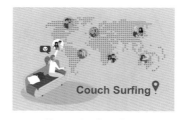
Couch Surfing

1. Which of the following would a backpacker most likely need?

(A)

(B)

Couch Surfing

(C)

R COMPANY

👤 Name: Sam Mitchell

🔗 Position: Personal Tour Guide

📍 Company: MyProGuide

📞 Tel: 0912-345-678

✉ Email: samisguide@myproguide.com

(D)

The Ultimate Tour Groups

How a tour group changes your life

Unit

14

跨
世
代

2. The sentences in paragraph 3 are numbered ❶ to ❹. Which sentence gives the definition of backpacker? Write down the **NUMBER** of the sentence below.

_____

3. Which of the following is **NOT** mentioned in the passage?

(A) The dangers of traveling alone.

(B) The benefits of couch surfing.

(C) Different ways of traveling without hiring a tour guide.

(D) The reasons why some young people prefer being backpackers.

4. What is the writer's attitude toward backpackers?

(A) Neutral.　　　　　　　(B) Negative.

(C) Persuasive.　　　　　　(D) Doubtful.

Check (✓) the possible characteristics of a package tour and backpacking based on the passage.

Characteristics	Package tour	Backpacking
1. Hire a tour guide.		
2. Find a tour agency.		
3. Use public transportation more.		
4. Book train tickets by themselves.		
5. Explore the world on foot.		
6. Have only a few necessary items in carry-on bags.		
7. Travel by getting free rides.		
8. Sleep at the local's house without paying.		
9. Stay in a luxury hotel more.		
10. Travel with heavy baggage.		

字彙實力

❶ **luxury hotel (n.)** 奢華旅館

❻ **hostel (n.)** 旅社

❷ **journey (n.)** 旅行

❼ **hitchhike (v.)** 免費搭便車旅行

❸ **travel agency (n.)** 旅行社

❽ **evolve (v.)** 逐漸演變

❹ **settle (v.)** 安排好

❾ **couch surfing (n.)** 沙發衝浪

❺ **arrangement (n.)** 安排

❿ **explore (v.)** 探索

延伸活動

WORD SUDOKU

Complete the box below. Each row, column, and 2×2 square of the box contains these four words: travel, hotel, hostel, baggage.

travel

hotel

hostel

baggage

hotel			
		travel	
			hostel
	hostel		

Unit 15 How Voice Recognition Technology Changes Our Lives

Have you ever imagined what computers will be like in the future? Will we still see images or watch videos on the computer screens? Will we still need to type? Through voice ¹recognition technology, ²keyboards would eventually become unnecessary.

Using voice recognition technology, or called VRT, is a ³dynamic process in which computers make many spoken languages into text. Some ⁴electronic devices such as smartphones are already equipped with VRT. Overall, the accuracy is great, but some devices still have trouble ⁵distinguishing names and words that sound similar. Another problem VRT developers face is ⁶accents. Two people speaking the same language can sound very different, depending on which region of a country they grew up in. However, as time goes on, researchers will gradually ⁷overcome these ⁸obstacles, and VRT will be able to understand any accent in the near future.

❶VRT is applied to not only electronic devices but also our houses. ❷When you are at the door of your room, you can simply say "Turn the lights on," and your room will be lit. ❸Instead of using a ⁹remote control, you can say "Turn on the TV and turn to a movie channel." ❹Then you can enjoy watching a movie. ❺All in all, the possibilities of VRT are ¹⁰endless, and it allows your imagination to go wild.

1. Which of the following can be inferred from this passage?

(A) Air conditioner can be turned on by robots.

(B) The spoken commands can be carried out.

(C) The spoken words cannot be interpreted.

(D) The text message can be sent by touching a screen.

2. Write down "true," "false," or "not given" for each of the following statements with the information contained in the passage.

statement	true / false / not given
(1) The accuracy of VRT has reached perfection.	(1) _____
(2) VRT allows your imagination to go wild.	(2) _____
(3) VRT will make smartphone users less smart.	(3) _____
(4) VRT only makes the English spoken words into text.	(4) _____
(5) VRT can help you control your TV without a remote control.	(5) _____

3. Where does this passage most likely appear?

(A) In a scientific journal.

(B) In a smartphone manual.

(C) On a website of a gallery.

(D) In an advertisement featuring the latest TV.

4. The sentences in paragraph 3 are numbered ❶ to ❺. Which sentence best indicates the author's attitude toward VRT? Write down the **NUMBER** of the sentence below.

_____

Unit

15

跨
世
代

Read the product descriptions given below. Which of the following does **NOT** apply the voice recognition technology?

(A) This user-friendly product is designed to listen to your words. You can use a simple sentence, for example, " 23°C."

(B) This is the latest TV. You may operate the TV without pushing any button. Functions such as power on and off and changing channels can all be performed by your voice.

(C) If you are a fan of video games, you probably know Xnect. This device may connect to your electronic equipment and allows you play games via motions and spoken words.

(D) This smartphone features a touch screen supported by the multi-touch technology. Therefore, a traditional keyboard is given up.

字彙實力

❶ **recognition (n.)** 辨識

❷ **keyboard (n.)** 鍵盤

❸ **dynamic (adj.)** 動態的

❹ **electronic (adj.)** 電子的

❺ **distinguish (v.)** 辨別

❻ **accent (n.)** 口音

❼ **overcome (v.)** 克服

❽ **obstacle (n.)** 阻礙

❾ **remote (adj.)** 遙控的

❿ **endless (adj.)** 無限的

延伸活動

Voice commands are usually imperative sentences (祈使句). Translate the following Chinese voice commands into English.

1.

開燈

(1) _____

關燈

(2) _____

2.

把音量調大

(1) _____

把音量調小

(2) _____

3.

開門

(1) _____

鎖門

(2) _____

Is Webcasting Entertainment or Brainwashing?

Whom are you following on ¹social media at this very moment? Is he or she a big eater eating like a horse, a ²techie ³unboxing the latest smartphone, or a model ⁴removing his or her ⁵makeup? Whomever you follow on social media is called an Internet celebrity or a social media influencer. He or she may make a "good" living by ⁶webcasting whatever he or she wants because nowadays everything can be used to make money!

The first webcast, produced by Apple in 1995, was an ⁷audio webcast of concerts in New York clubs for entertainment. Later, rock bands used it to broadcast **live** concerts on the Internet. So far, almost everyone can webcast anything anytime around the world. Whoever has a smartphone or a computer can share whichever theme he or she is interested in online.

❶ Webcasting has also become an important part of business. ❷ Some companies webcast meetings, ⁸conferences, and training videos. ❸ Others use this technology for sales and marketing. ❹ Furthermore, education has also been greatly affected by webcasting. ❺ Students don't have to be in the classroom and be in class. ❻ This helps encourage self-learning or even lifelong learning. ❼ What's more, webcasting has also influenced elections and even voters' decisions. ❽ Many politicians have social media ⁹accounts and produce webcasts regularly to share their policies or even lives. ❾ By interacting with the audience, they hope to win the voters' trust and the election.

Apparently, what started as a form of entertainment has now influenced the way we act, the way we learn, and even the way we think. Therefore, be careful not to be ¹⁰fooled by millions of webcasters!

1. What does "**live**" refer to in the second paragraph?

   (A) Being alive.

   (B) Being able to explode.

   (C) Being important at the moment.

   (D) Being watched while the event is happening.

2. What is the third paragraph mainly about?

   (A) How to become a webcaster.

   (B) How webcasting affects our life.

   (C) Why webcasting cannot brainwash us.

   (D) Why webcasting is becoming unpopular.

3. The sentences in paragraph 3 are numbered ❶ to ❾. Which sentence best describes the picture below? Write down the **NUMBER** of the sentence below.

Unit

16

跨
世
代

4. Which of the following is most likely a scene where people create a webcast with a smartphone?

   (A)   (B)

   (C)   (D)

Look at the pie charts below. Which of the following statements is true?

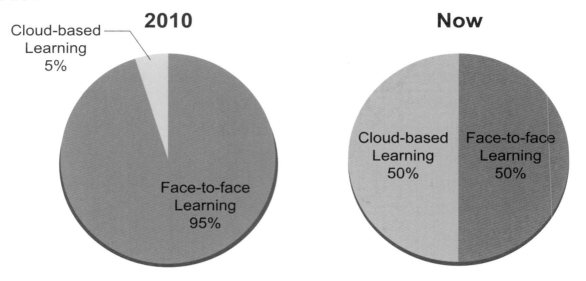

(A) Face-to-face learning has been developed recently.

(B) Face-to-face learning is the mainstream education now.

(C) The percentage of people using cloud-based learning has increased.

(D) The share of cloud-based learning is greater than that of face-to-face learning now.

字彙實力

❶ social media (n.) 社群媒體   ❻ webcast (v.) 網路直播

❷ techie (n.) 科技迷   ❼ audio (adj.) 聲音的

❸ unbox (v.) 開箱 (網路常用語)   ❽ conference (n.) 會議

❹ remove (v.) 卸除   ❾ account (n.) 帳戶

❺ makeup (n.) 妝   ❿ fool (v.) 愚弄

延伸活動

Fill in each blank with the correct word from the box. Make changes if necessary.

whatever	whenever	wherever	whoever
whomever		whichever	however

1. _____ passes the test will be awarded.

2. A spoiled child always does _____ he / she wants.

3. We can go _____ you like today because it's your birthday.

4. You should be polite to _____ your talk to in the conference.

5. _____ the baby is hungry, the parents feed it right away.

6. You can come to have a talk with me _____ you have difficulties.

7. Since it is your housewarming party, you can invite _____ you like.

8. Mom can choose _____ she likes, a pearl necklace or a gold bracelet.

9. _____ hard Kelly studies, she always falls behind with her schoolwork.

10. The little boy shows no interest in basketball games, _____ exciting they may be.

Knowledge is a city to the building of which every human being brought a stone.

—*Ralph Waldo Emerson*

跨領域

Cross Disciplines

知識是一座城堡，每個人都應為它增磚添瓦。

——拉爾夫・沃爾多・愛默生

Unit 17 The Origins of Fingerprint Identification

If you have ever watched any crime films or murder [1]mysteries on television, you may have noticed that police officers always search for [2]evidence at the crime scene. One of the most important clues to the identity of the criminals is the [3]fingerprints left at the scene. However, how did people start looking for fingerprints and [4]cite them as evidence in the first place? Here is the story of the first crime solved due to fingerprints.

❶ It all started in 1892 in Argentina. ❷ One day, two young children got brutally murdered in their own home. ❸There were two **suspects**. ❹One was the children's mother, Francisca Rojas, and the other was their neighbor, Pedro Ramón Velázquez. ❺Both [5]denied having committed murder. ❻After a few days, one officer, Eduardo Alvárez, was sent there to help carry out this [6]investigation. ❼He found a single bloody fingerprint in the bedroom. ❽ Instead of wiping it away, Alvárez decided to collect this evidence and compared it with the two suspects' fingerprints. ❾The police contacted Juan Vucetich who was working on fingerprint [7]classification in order to identify these fingerprints. ❿ In the end, Francisca Rojas was proven to be guilty. ⓫ She [8]confessed that one of her dates wanted to marry her, but he didn't like her children. ⓬Therefore, she chose to take her children's life.

The method of fingerprint identification proved to be so [9]effective that the police around the world have been using it ever since. With the development of technology, detectives can now accurately [10]match fingerprints and find the criminals immediately.

混合題型

1. How does the author begin the passage?

   (A) By giving a question.

   (B) By giving a definition.

   (C) By providing statistics.

   (D) By mentioning a murder case.

2. What does the word "**suspect**" in the second paragraph most likely mean?

   (A) A person whose job is to fight crime.

   (B) A person who is badly hurt or killed.

   (C) A person who decides how criminals are punished.

   (D) A person who is believed to have committed a crime.

3. Below are the plots of the crime in the second paragraph. In what order does the author talk about the story?

   a. The mother was proven to be guilty.

   b. One day, two children were killed in their own home.

   c. One police inspector found a single bloody fingerprint in the bedroom and decided to compare it with the two suspects' fingerprints.

   d. There were two suspects, the children's mother and their neighbor. Both denied having committed murder.

   (A) c → a → b → d.　　　　(B) b → d → c → a.

   (C) a → d → c → b.　　　　(D) c → d → b → a.

4. The sentences in paragraph 2 are numbered ❶ to ⓬. Which sentence best indicates the killer's motive? Write down the **NUMBER** of the sentence below.

   _____

Unit

17

跨
領
域

Which of the following purposes of fingerprint identification is **NOT** mentioned in this passage?

(A)

(B)

(C)

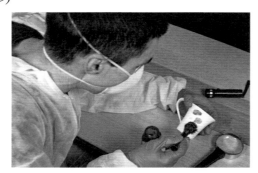

(D)

字彙實力

❶ **mystery (n.)** 懸疑劇

❻ **investigation (n.)** 調查

❷ **evidence (n.)** 證據

❼ **classification (n.)** 分類

❸ **fingerprint (n.)** 指紋

❽ **confess (v.)** 坦承

❹ **cite (v.)** 引證

❾ **effective (adj.)** 有效的

❺ **deny (v.)** 否認

❿ **match (v.)** 配對

延伸活動

Check (✓) the facts about the crime mentioned in the passage.

☐ 1. It began in 1892 in Armenia.

☐ 2. Two young children got brutally murdered at home.

☐ 3. There were three suspects.

☐ 4. The suspects are Francisca Rojas and Pedro Ramón Velázquez.

☐ 5. Eduardo Alvárez helped carry out this investigation.

☐ 6. Juan Vucetich found a single bloody fingerprint in the bedroom.

☐ 7. Alvárez decided to wipe the fingerprint away.

☐ 8. Juan Vucetich worked on fingerprint classification.

☐ 9. Pedro Ramón Velázquez was proven to be guilty.

☐ 10. Francisca Rojas confessed to the murder.

Unit

17

跨
領
域

Unit 18 The Unknown Part of "The Road Not Taken"

The United States has a long tradition of ¹poetry. Walt Whitman, the father of free verse, celebrated ²democracy and freedom like no other. As a poet, Sylvia Plath was well ahead of her time. She explored male ³domination and even death. **So far, the poets are numerous as the stars in the sky.** But which poem is most popular of all time? That ⁴belongs to "The Road Not Taken" by Robert Frost. Frost was a master at writing poems about isolation, countryside, and daily life.

For most people, the main message of this poem is that life is filled with many choices, and the decisions will certainly affect the following paths. Once we make a decision, there will be no going back. Later in life, we may look back and wonder what life might have become if we had chosen differently. This explanation ⁵makes perfect sense. Of course we have to make choices in life, and it goes without saying that those choices will influence what job we get, where we live, who we love, and so on.

But is that really what the poem is about? No! As it ⁶turns out, "The Road Not Taken" is ⁷plain. Although many people tend to think too much about the ⁸abstract meaning of the poem, the real story behind it is as follows. During the period when Frost lived in the English countryside, he often went hiking with his friend, Edward Thomas. However, Thomas would often ⁹regret the routes chosen among those hikes. This inspired Frost to write "The Road Not Taken" about those roads they might have walked down. Nevertheless, this poem makes a ¹⁰considerable impact on many people and is considered one of the most popular poems of all time.

混合題型

1. Why does the author mention Walt Whitman and Sylvia Plath in this passage?

   (A) They are both famous American poets.

   (B) They are more famous than Robert Frost.

   (C) They often went hiking with Robert Frost.

   (D) They interpreted Robert Frost's poem in a plain way.

2. What does the author mean by "**So far, the poets are numerous as the stars in the sky.**" in the first paragraph?

   (A) The poets get star quality.

   (B) Many of the American poems talk about stars.

   (C) There are countless poets in American history.

   (D) The poets are always inspired by the stars in the sky.

3. According to the third paragraph, which of the following comments is true about "The Road Not Taken"?

   (A) Jill : It is a poem that almost everyone misunderstands.

   👍 159 👎 1   REPLY

   (B) Ben: This poem is about death and male domination.

   👍 148 👎 3   REPLY

   (C) Roy: The purpose of this poem is to describe the isolation of the countryside.

   👍 199 👎 2   REPLY

   (D) Amy: "The Road Not Taken" is a masterpiece and it talks about democracy and freedom in the United States.

   👍 315 👎 1   REPLY

Unit

18

跨
領
域

4. Fill in the blanks with the information contained in the passage about these famous poets.

	theme(s) of poems
Walt Whitman	_____
Sylvia Plath	male domination and even death
Robert Frost	_____

進階練習

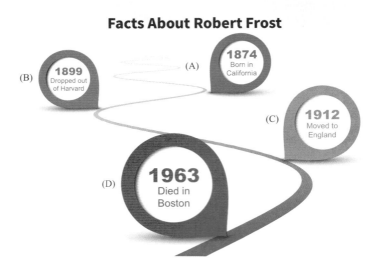

Facts About Robert Frost

(A)

(B) **1899** Dropped out of Harvard

1874 Born in California

(C) **1912** Moved to England

(D) **1963** Died in Boston

According to the passage, when did Robert Frost most likely write the poem "The Road Not Taken"?

(A) A (B) B (C) C (D) D

字彙實力

❶ **poetry (n.)** 詩作

❻ **turn out (phr.)** 結果是

❷ **democracy (n.)** 民主

❼ **plain (adj.)** 簡單的

❸ **domination (n.)** 主宰

❽ **abstract (adj.)** 抽象的

❹ **belong to (phr.)** 屬於

❾ **regret (v.)** 懊悔

❺ **make sense (phr.)** 有道理

❿ **considerable (adj.)** 相當大的

Look at the following clues and fill the white squares with letters that form words (which are mentioned in the passage). Then, find the hidden word in the red rectangle.

Clues:

1. A choice that someone makes after thinking carefully.

2. A person who writes poems.

3. A great number of.

4. Liked or enjoyed by lots of people.

5. Existing as an idea, feeling, or quality instead of a physical one.

6. To feel sorry about what you have done or have not done.

7. The state of being alone and feeling unhappy.

8. Land outside cities and towns.

9. Happening on every day.

Unit

18

跨
領
域

⑩ The hidden word is: _____

85

Nessie: Reality or Fiction?

People say it looks like an elephant, a dragon, a giant snake-like fish, and many more animals. It is said that the [1]creature was first spotted in 565 AD in Scotland. Later, the creature was widely reported after it was seen during the 1930s. No one knows if it is real or just a mystery. It is the Loch Ness Monster, [2]nicknamed Nessie.

In July 1933, a couple claimed they had seen a large creature crossing the road in front of their car while driving along the Loch Ness. They said it was about 1.2 meters high and 7.6 meters long. Furthermore, its long neck was similar to an elephant's [3]trunk. A local newspaper reported the story and it spread quickly. A year later, another man took a picture of a monster rising out of the lake, but it was later proven **false**. Nevertheless, all of this [4]publicity made people from all over the world want to see Nessie. They began traveling to the lake, hoping to catch a glimpse of the mysterious monster.

❶Since 1933, there have been many reported sightings of the Loch Ness Monster. ❷Many people [5]mistook deer, seals, waves, and even [6]logs for Nessie. ❸ Researchers have also tried to use technology to find any evidence of Nessie but only succeeded in finding some underwater creatures and more than 3,000 [7]bacteria so far. ❹Although most scientists believe that Nessie does not [8]exist at all, some people still think it might be one kind of undiscovered [9]dinosaur. ❺The Loch Ness Monster in the Highlands remains a mysterious [10]legend yet to be solved.

混合題型

1. What does "**false**" mean in the second paragraph?

    (A) Fake.   (B) Imaginative.

    (C) Real.   (D) Mysterious.

2. Which of the following looks most similar to the monster described in the second paragraph?

(A)

(B)

(C)

(D)

Unit

19

跨領域

3. According to the passage, which of the following is true about the Loch Ness Monster?

    (A) It has an elephant's trunk.

    (B) It was first spotted in Switzerland.

    (C) It was widely reported during the 1930s.

    (D) It was about 7.6 meters high and 1.2 meters long.

4. The sentences in paragraph 3 are numbered ❶ to ❺. Which sentence best indicates the author's attitude toward Nessie? Write down the **NUMBER** of the sentence below.

The following is a map of the United Kingdom. Mark the place where the Loch Ness Monster was spotted with the letters. For example, London lies within the square "Cg."

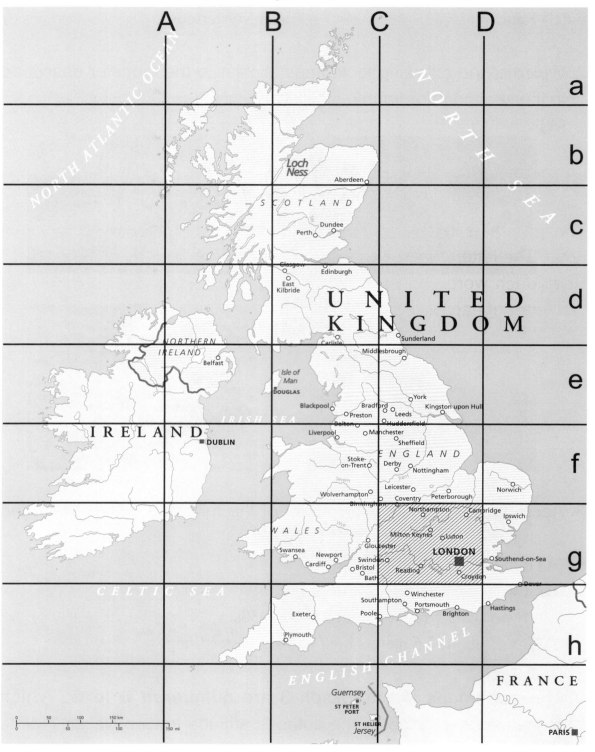

Answer: _____

字彙實力

❶ **creature (n.)** 生物

❷ **nickname (v.)** 給…起綽號

❸ **trunk (n.)** 象鼻

❹ **publicity (n.)** (媒體的) 關注，宣傳

❺ **mistake (v.)** 誤認

❻ **log (n.)** 圓木

❼ **bacteria (n. pl.)** 細菌

❽ **exist (v.)** 存在

❾ **dinosaur (n.)** 恐龍

❿ **legend (n.)** 傳說

延伸活動

The letter "t" is in the center of the flower and other letters are on each petal. The letters on the same petal can form a word with the letter "t." Spell each word shown in the passage in the following blanks. The first letter of each word is shown below.

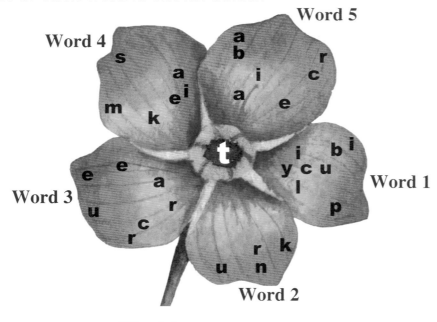

Word 1: p _____

Word 2: t _____

Word 3: c _____

Word 4: m_____

Word 5: b _____

What place is home to more than 1,500 [1]species, such as fish, whales, sharks, dolphins, sea turtles, and many other sea animals? What is one of the largest living [2]organisms on earth that can be seen from outer space? Which [3]ecosystem [4]consists of 2,900 individual live [5]coral reefs and 900 islands? It is the Great Barrier Reef, considered one of the seven natural wonders of the world.

❶The Great Barrier Reef is located off the northeast coast of Australia. ❷It is almost ten times bigger than Taiwan and is just slightly smaller than Japan. ❸Sightseeing is so popular here because the water surrounding the reef is clear enough to see the magnificent underwater creatures. ❹Each year, the Great Barrier Reef attracts millions of tourists coming to see some of the most beautiful sea creatures in the world and explore the colorful coral reefs. ❺Tourism helps the Australian economy grow and educates the public about this great natural wonder.

But the future of the Great Barrier Reef is uncertain. Human activities, such as walking on the coral reefs and keeping pieces of coral as souvenirs, are [6]damaging the coral reefs. Apart from that, climate change poses a major [7]threat. Apparently, climate emergency [8]arises. It causes the ocean water to become warmer, which is leading to mass [9]bleaching of coral reefs. Coral reefs gradually lose color, turn white and then die from [10]marine heat waves. Scientists have warned that if global warming continues, we will lose a natural wonder of the world in the near future.

Before

After

1. Which of the following is **NOT** mentioned as a threat to the Great Barrier Reef?

(A) Whales and sharks.

(B) Climate change.

(C) Human activities.

(D) Marine heat waves.

2. The sentences in paragraph 2 are numbered ❶ to ❺. Which sentence best describes the size of the Great Barrier Reef? Write down the **NUMBER** of the sentence below.

_____

3. According to the passage, where is the Great Barrier Reef located? Choose the English letter linked to the state.

(A) A   (B) B   (C) C   (D) D

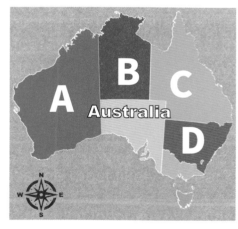

4. How does the author conclude the passage in the last paragraph?

(A) By issuing a warning.

(B) By mentioning an incident.

(C) By providing statistics.

(D) By comparing scientists' responses.

Unit

20

跨
領
域

The following bar chart is the average sea surface temperature. Which of the following can be inferred from the passage and the bar chart?

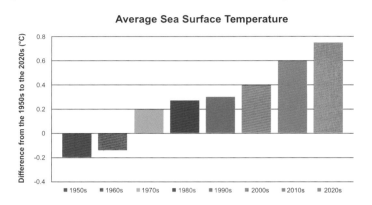

(A)

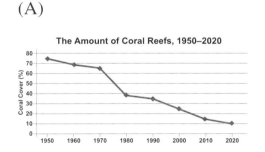

(B)

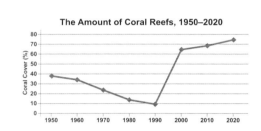

(C)

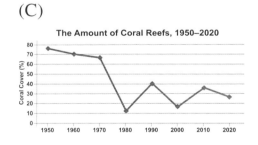

(D)

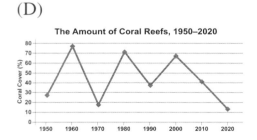

字彙實力

❶ **species (n.)** 物種　　　　　❻ **damage (v.)** 傷害

❷ **organism (n.)** 有機體　　　❼ **threat (n.)** 威脅

❸ **ecosystem (n.)** 生態系統　❽ **arise (v.)** 發生

❹ **consist of (phr.)** 由…組成　❾ **bleach (v.)** 白化

❺ **coral reef (n.)** 珊瑚礁　　　❿ **marine (adj.)** 海洋的

延伸活動

According to the passage, fill in the blanks with the options given below. Match the words to the correct definitions.

Words:

_____	1. island
_____	2. future
_____	3. cause
_____	4. educate
_____	5. natural
_____	6. colorful

Unit

20

跨領域

Definitions:

(A) The time that will come.
(B) Teach someone about something.
(C) Bright in color or having different colors.
(D) Existing in nature and not controlled by people.
(E) To make something happen, especially something bad.
(F) A piece of land that is completely surrounded by water.

Unit 21 Gender Roles of the Animal Kingdom

❶ If you think gender roles only exist in the human world, think again. ❷ In the animal ¹kingdom, males and females have their own ²complicated problems to deal with, so at least we are not alone. ❸ Let's start with the obvious ³feature first—body size. ❹ Among birds and ⁴mammals, males are larger than females on average. ❺ This is because males are often the ones who have to fight for food, and additionally have to be able to attract mates as well.

Usually in the animal kingdom, the larger the males are, the easier for them to find their partners. In order to win their mates, many species have found ways to ⁵exaggerate their body sizes. For example, they make a deep sound in order to show that they are larger than they actually are. If some females are fooled, they would believe that they have the strongest or largest males they could possibly find. Male lions, koalas, and red deer have all been found to sound louder than they are to attract females.

On the other hand, when it comes to raising babies, gender plays a major role in the animal kingdom as well. Generally, it is moms who take care of eggs. However, for **emperor penguins**, it is just the opposite. After females ⁶lay their eggs, it is moms who ⁷head toward sea in search of food. Meanwhile, stay-at-home dads sit on their eggs for almost three months without eating anything. Therefore, it is not only females who make great ⁸sacrifices to ⁹bring up their children. Males also play important roles in ¹⁰looking after their babies.

1. What is the passage mainly about?

(A) Whether penguins have gender differences.

(B) How gender roles play in the animal kingdom.

(C) What makes human beings differ from lions, koalas, and deer.

(D) Why different body sizes are essential for lions, koalas, and deer.

2. The sentences in paragraph 1 are numbered ❶ to ❺. Which sentence best explains the reason why males are larger than females on average? Write down the **NUMBER** of the sentence below.

_____

3. Why is "**emperor penguins**" mentioned in the third paragraph?

(A) To show an exception that only females take care of kids.

(B) To convince readers that gender roles only exist in the human world.

(C) To prove that penguins are just the same with lions, koalas, and deer.

(D) To support the theory that males sound louder to protect family.

4. Write down "true," "false," or "not given" for each of the following statements with the information contained in the passage.

statement	true / false / not given
(1) Male koalas sound louder to attract females.	(1) _____
(2) Males have bigger body sizes only to fight for food.	(2) _____
(3) Female red deer with a bigger body size cannot attract mates.	(3) _____
(4) Male lions have been found to sound louder to win their mates.	(4) _____
(5) Male emperor penguins sit on eggs while females leave to hunt for food.	(5) _____

Unit

21

跨
領
域

Which of the following facts is most likely to be one of the examples in the third paragraph?

Facts About Seahorses

(A) A seahorse is not a horse. It is fish that has fins and a curly tail.

(B) Seahorses can change their colors to escape from enemies.

(C) Male seahorses have brood pouches (育兒袋) on their bellies to carry eggs.

(D) A male seahorse attracts a female by dancing and showing his empty pouch.

seahorse

字彙實力

❶ **kingdom (n.)** (動物、植物、礦物) 界	❻ **lay (v.)** 產蛋
❷ **complicated (adj.)** 複雜的	❼ **head (v.)** 前往 (某方向)
❸ **feature (n.)** 特徵	❽ **sacrifice (n.)** 犧牲
❹ **mammal (n.)** 哺乳動物	❾ **bring up (phr.)** 養育
❺ **exaggerate (v.)** 誇大	❿ **look after (phr.)** 照顧

延伸活動

Each across and down word has a clue. Look at the following clues, solve the puzzle, and write down the words (which are mentioned in the passage). Some of them have been done for you.

Clues:

Across	**Down**
① A bird that cannot fly but swim.	Ⓐ A woman or a girl.
② The condition of being a male or female.	Ⓑ To make something greater in size or degree than it really is.
③ A man or a boy.	Ⓒ Living things other than plants.
④ Difficult to understand and deal with.	Ⓓ To produce eggs from the body.

Unit

21

跨
領
域

97

Going Green Is in Fashion

❶In the 1990s, several supermodels posed ¹naked in order to take action and speak up. ❷They felt great sympathy for animals raised and killed for their ²fur. ❸Furthermore, they also felt ³disgust for those who used fur to make ⁴designer clothes. ❹Therefore, these supermodels said that they would rather go on stage without clothes than wear furs. ❺This publicity campaign worked. ❻Wearing furs was no longer cool, but going green or so called "eco-fashion" was.

Today, refusing using fur is not enough. It is even more important for designers to understand how the materials used to make clothes are produced. Is the cotton grown ⁵organically? Are the workers in ⁶garment factories under fair working conditions? It is also extremely important that products are ⁷manufactured according to the ⁸principle of "fair trade." Many designers also pride themselves on applying recycled materials, such as metal, paper, and old rubber tires, to their designs.

Although many designers are changing their ways, there are still many large companies refusing to adopt green practices. "Fast fashion" encourages people to buy more new clothes, be dressed in the latest fashion, and then throw them away immediately. Lots of ⁹wearable clothes are dumped and become garbage.

"Going green" is growing popular, but some people ¹⁰are still fond of the cheap and fashionable clothes instead of the environment-friendly products. **For the sake of** the planet Earth, hopefully the eco-friendly products will become the major trend soon.

混合題型

1. What is the purpose of this passage?

   (A) To explain how supermodels choose materials for their clothes.

   (B) To illustrate how "fair trade" has changed the international business.

   (C) To describe how eco-friendly ideas influence the clothing market.

   (D) To prove that fast fashion has little impact on our environment.

2. The sentences in paragraph 1 are numbered ❶ to ❻. Which sentence best indicates the author's attitude toward eco-fashion? Write down the **NUMBER** of the sentence below.

   _____

3. Which of the following is **NOT** mentioned as an example of "eco-fashion" in the second paragraph?

   (A)

   (B)

   (C)

   (D)

Unit

22

跨
領
域

4. Which is closest in meaning to the phrase "**for the sake of**" in the last paragraph?

   (A) For the benefit of.　　　(B) To make use of.

   (C) As a result of.　　　　(D) By means of.

Check (✓) the possible characteristics of eco-fashion and fast fashion based on the passage.

Characteristics	Eco-fashion	Fast fashion
1. Contain recycled materials.		
2. Keep up with the latest fashion.		
3. Persuade customers to buy more.		
4. Encourage people to throw old clothes.		
5. Produce cheaper clothes.		
6. Use eco-friendly materials.		
7. Create more garbage.		

字彙實力

❶ naked (adj.) 裸露的

❷ fur (n.) 毛皮

❸ disgust (n.) 憎惡

❹ designer clothes (n.) 名牌服裝

❺ organically (adv.) 有機地

❻ garment (n.) 衣服

❼ manufacture (v.) 製作

❽ principle (n.) 原則

❾ wearable (adj.) 可以穿的

❿ be fond of (phr.) 喜愛

延伸活動

It is (adj.) for (sb) to (v.)

An example in the passage:

It is <u>even more important</u> for <u>designers</u> to <u>understand</u> how the materials
       (adj.)   (sb)   (v.)

used to make clothes are produced.

Look at the following pictures. Make sentences by putting the given words in the right order.

1. (for a man / in the river / It is dangerous / to swim alone)

_____ .

2. (exercise / the elderly to / It is / healthy for / regularly)

_____ .

3. (recommended / for people / It is not / to overeat)

_____ .

Unit

22

跨
領
域

Unit 23 Experiencing the Outside World

Thomas Friedman wrote a book named *The World Is Flat*, in which he described how countries influenced one another heavily and eventually ¹blurred the ²borders between countries. Thus, as citizens of the global village, it is especially important for us to do more than just learn from books. The key is to experience different cultures and always have ³enthusiasm for learning.

❶In order to broaden the mind, many students take time to see the world. ❷Some of them take a gap year to travel abroad before going to college. ❸Taking a gap year allows the students to learn about other cultures personally. ❹An experience like this can be valuable, and it may also make the students become more ⁴mature than those who don't take a gap year. ❺ However, for those who go straight from high school to college, they can still gain considerable experience by studying abroad in the summer or winter vacation or being an exchange student. ❻ They can also have plenty of ⁵opportunities to learn foreign languages, make friends from different ⁶backgrounds, and communicate with the local people. ❼ Some of them even apply for a ⁷homestay. ❽This helps them learn ⁸the ins and outs of the daily life of the local family.

No matter what kind of job you want in the future, experiencing the outside world can be helpful. It cannot only ⁹sharpen your language skills but also expand your ¹⁰horizons. This can **translate into** a better job, more interests or a more fulfilling life experience.

混合題型

1. Why is "**Thomas Friedman**" mentioned in the first paragraph?

(A) To point out the reason why he wrote this article.

(B) To persuade readers to learn beyond books.

(C) To give an example of being an exchange student.

(D) To describe the man who explores the world in his gap year.

2. According to the passage, which of the following is **NOT** mentioned as a way to experience the outside world?

(A)

(B)

(C)

(D)

3. The sentences in paragraph 2 are numbered ❶ to ❽. Which sentence best indicates the advantage of applying for a homestay? Write down the **NUMBER** of the sentence below.

_____

4. What does "**translate into**" in the last paragraph refer to?

(A) To interpret word meanings.

(B) To make a situation happen.

(C) To make a promise of something.

(D) To get knowledge from something.

Unit

23

跨
領
域

The following bar chart shows the number of participants who have attended Sanmin gap year fair. Which of the following can be inferred from the bar chart?

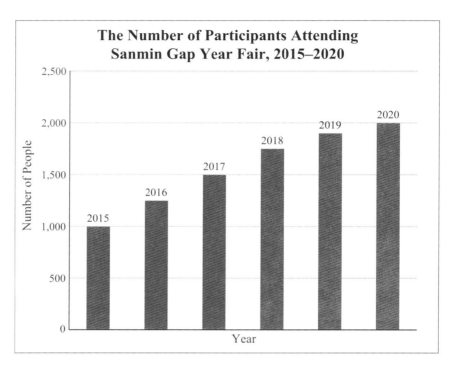

(A) Less people are interested in joining summer camps over the years.

(B) The number of people studying abroad has decreased over the years.

(C) The number of people taking a gap year remains the same over the years.

(D) The number of people attending this gap year fair has increased in these years.

字彙實力

❶ blur (v.) 模糊　　　　　　　❻ background (n.) 背景

❷ border (n.) 邊界　　　　　　❼ homestay (n.) 寄宿家庭

❸ enthusiasm (n.) 熱情　　　　❽ the ins and outs (n.) 細項

❹ mature (adj.) 成熟的　　　　❾ sharpen (v.) 改善

❺ opportunity (n.) 機會　　　　❿ horizon (n.) 眼界

延伸活動

not only . . . but also . . .

An example in the passage:

It cannot only sharpen your language skills but also expand your horizons.

Combine the two sentences into one by using "not only . . . but also . . ."

1. Hard work is the key to success.

   Preparation is the key to success.

⇒ _____

2. The fear of the flu has led to the panic buying of masks.

   The fear of the flu has led to a steep drop in business.

⇒ _____

3. The international book fair appealed to those who love to read.

   The international book fair appealed to those who don't love to read.

⇒ _____

Unit

23

跨
領
域

Unit 24 What Is Your Learning Style?

Imagine that you are given the choice between two different classes. In class A, you are required to sit at a school desk and listen to lectures. In class B, the teacher hands you some tools, divides you and the classmates into groups, sets a timer, and asks you to complete a piece of work together within the next 30 minutes. You can either sit back and listen or join in the discussions and try your best. Which class would you choose?

Each type of class has its advantages. In class A, a lecture-based class, students can gain [1]a good deal of information in a short time. They are responsible for listening carefully to the lesson. However, this learning style has its [2]limitations. For example, the students may be used to [3]memorizing facts without critically thinking about the issues. As a result, the students might be able to pass [4]multiple-choice tests, but struggle to answer open questions.

In class B, students have the opportunity to work with the materials [5]directly. They can learn a great deal through class discussions, [6]experiments and [7]cooperation. Nevertheless, one major disadvantage of this learning style is that students' performance is highly [8]associated with the classroom atmosphere. If it is hard to keep the class in order, the students may find it difficult to learn.

Both approaches can be [9]adapted to suit the needs of the individuals. If you are stuck in a class, join a small study group and discuss together. If [10]hands-on experience doesn't help you, spend more time studying thoroughly instead. There is no wrong way to learn!

A Lecture-based Class

A Discussion-based Class

VS

1. How is the information about learning styles organized in paragraphs 2 to 3?

    (A) By cause and effect.   (B) In the sequence of time.

    (C) By giving pros and cons.   (D) In order of importance.

2. Which of the following best describes the author's attitude toward two different learning styles?

    (A) Neutral.

    (B) Doubtful.

    (C) Defensive.

    (D) Amazed.

3. Which of the following can be inferred from the check list?

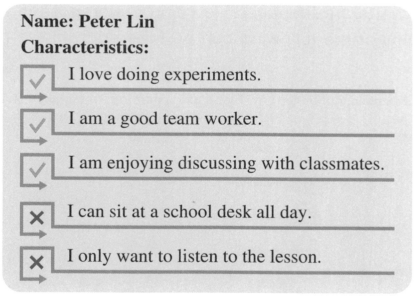

    (A) Class A is suitable for Peter.

    (B) Class B is suitable for Peter.

    (C) Both of class A and class B are suitable for Peter.

    (D) None of class A and class B is suitable for Peter.

Unit

24

跨
領
域

4. Fill in the blanks with the information contained in the passage about class A and class B.

	advantage(s)	disadvantage(s)
class A	1. gain _____ in a short time 2. They are responsible for listening carefully to the lesson.	1. without <u>critically thinking</u> about the issues 2. struggle to answer open questions
class B	1. work with the materials directly 2. learn a great deal through _____	students' performance is highly associated with the _____

📎 **進階練習**

The following pie charts are teenagers' learning preferences in the past and now. Which of the following can be inferred from the pie charts?

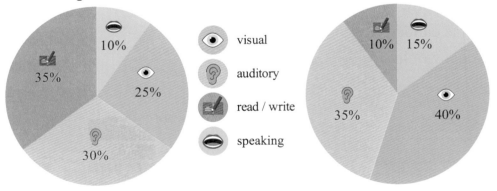

Teenagers' Learning Preferences in the Past

Teenagers' Learning Preferences Now

(A) Currently, speaking is teenagers' favorite currently.

(B) Teenagers show more interest in reading books now.

(C) More teenagers like to learn through videos and pictures nowadays.

(D) Today, teenagers are willing to spend more time on reading and writing.

字彙實力

❶ **a good deal of** (phr.) 大量

❻ **experiment** (n.) 實驗

❷ **limitation** (n.) 限制

❼ **cooperation** (n.) 合作

❸ **memorize** (v.) 記憶

❽ **associated** (adj.) 相關的

❹ **multiple-choice** (adj.) 多項選擇題的

❾ **adapt** (v.) 調整

❺ **directly** (adv.) 直接地

❿ **hands-on** (adj.) 實際操作的

延伸活動

Here are some features of "lecture-based classes" and "discussion-based classes." Put them (A–F) into the correct category.

(A) Students can obtain lots of information shortly.

(B) Students can do some experiments.

(C) Students may lack the ability to think critically.

(D) Students might struggle to answer open questions.

(E) Students can learn a lot through class discussions.

(F) Students would have more chances to work together.

Unit

24

跨領域

Lecture-based Classes	**Discussion-based Classes**

國家圖書館出版品預行編目資料

跨閱英文／王信雲編著.－－初版二刷.－－臺北市：
三民，2024
　　面；　　公分.－－（Reading Power系列）

　　ISBN 978-957-14-6973-7　（平裝）
　　1. 英語 2. 讀本

805.18　　　　　　　　　　　　　　　109015660

 Reading Power 系列

跨閱英文

編 著 者	王信雲
審　　 定	車畇庭

創 辦 人	劉振強
發 行 人	劉仲傑
出 版 者	三民書局股份有限公司 (成立於 1953 年)

三民網路書店
https://www.sanmin.com.tw

地　　　址	臺北市復興北路 386 號　　（復北門市）　(02)2500-6600
	臺北市重慶南路一段 61 號 (重南門市)　(02)2361-7511
出 版 日 期	初版一刷 2021 年 1 月
	初版二刷 2024 年 8 月
書籍編號	S870680
I S B N	978-957-14-6973-7

三民書局

Reading Power 系列

Intermediate

111學年度起學科能力測驗、全民英檢中級適用

跨閱英文

Read Across Boundaries

翻譯與解析

王信雲　編著
車昀庭　審定

三民書局

Contents

Superstitions Related to Different Religions

迷信和不同宗教的關係

課文中譯

世上有許多宗教，各有各的信仰。經過數百年，部分強烈的信仰已經變成了迷信。

當談到基督教相關的迷信，部分信徒相信走在梯子下會帶來惡運。當梯子靠在牆壁上，梯子、牆和地面形成一個三角形。簡單三角形能代表什麼？在基督教的信仰裡，三角形代表神聖的三位一體，即聖父、聖子和聖靈。如果你走在梯子下，會被視為對上帝無禮。因此，你可能會遇到不好的事。

佛教相關的迷信是怎樣的呢？他們相信種什麼因，得什麼果。換句話說，如果做好事，以後會有好報。要是做了壞事，以後也會有惡報。它教你要為自己的行為負責。

最後，打呵欠不掩嘴，不僅沒禮貌，也是件危險的事。邪惡的靈魂正等你在打呵欠時，進入你的體內。因此，打呵欠掩嘴在伊斯蘭教國家是必要的事。另一個伊斯蘭教相關的迷信是，除非蜘蛛想要傷害你，否則你不該殺害牠們。那是因為蜘蛛曾經幫助先知穆罕默德逃跑，躲過追他的人。

你相信宗教上的迷信嗎？很難證明這些迷信是否真能帶來好運或惡運，但我們應該尊重它們。

混合題型

1. D　2. C　3. C　4. ❺

解析 1. (A) 圖根據第四段第四句和第五句的敘述，提到蜘蛛曾經幫助先知穆罕默德躲避敵人的追捕有功，所以除非必要，穆斯林不會殺害蜘蛛；(B) 圖根據第四段第一句和第二句提到打呵欠時如果不掩嘴，邪惡的靈魂就會趁虛而入；(C) 圖根據第二段第一句提到走在梯子下會帶來惡運；(D) 圖十三號星期五未在本文中出現，故本題答案為 (D)。

2. 由第五段第二句來看，作者認為雖然很難證明文中提到的行為是否真能帶來好運或惡運，但我們應該尊重所有不同和宗教相關的迷信，由此可知作者對於迷信抱持著 (C) 客觀的態度。

3. 作者於第二段、第三段和第四段分別舉出基督教、佛教和伊斯蘭教的迷信行為來佐證不同迷信和不同宗教的關係，故本題答案為 (C)。

4. 第四段❺提到穆斯林避免殺害蜘蛛的原因是蜘蛛曾經幫助先知穆罕默德逃跑，躲過追他的人。

進階練習　B

解析 文中提到日本人認為在火馬年出生的女性會剋夫，因此 1966 火馬年的出生率驟降，由本圖表來看，A 年、C 年、D 年皆無驟變，而 B 年的出生率驟降，故可推定 B 年為火馬年。

延伸活動

1. D　2. A　3. C　4. E　5. B　6. F

課文中譯

豐收慶祝活動是為了表示知足及感謝一切。在美國，它被稱為「感恩節」。在臺灣，阿美族部落慶祝「豐年祭」。在德國，它被取名為「豐收節」。在韓國，他們稱它「秋夕」。在西非，像是迦納和奈及利亞，「山藥節」是豐收慶祝活動的名稱。

儘管是不同的名字，食物在豐收慶祝活動中都扮演一個重要的角色。豐收意味著桌上有足夠的食物給每個人。所以，人們對上帝或他們的祖先幫助帶來收成表示感謝。同時，人們和家人及親戚享用和分享食物。人們慶祝節日的方式各不相同。它可以包含唱歌、跳舞、遊行或甚至放煙火。對於阿美族的豐年祭，傳統歌舞是必要的。在德國，這段時間裡，人們在教堂讚頌敬拜上帝。在某些國家，像是美國，感恩節只有一天。但在韓國，秋夕則持續幾天。

儘管依據不同的文化，習俗可能各不相同，但在這個特殊的日子，感恩的想法在全球各地都是一樣的。

混合題型

1. D　2. B　3. B　4.

	how people call their harvest celebrations
the United States	Thanksgiving Day
the Amis tribes	Harvest Festival
Germany	Erntedankfest
Korea	Chuseok
Ghana	Yam Festival
Nigeria	Yam Festival

解析 1. 本文主旨在於介紹各國豐收慶祝活動的名稱和慶祝方式，故本題答案為 (D)。
2. 第一段最後一句提到在西非，像是迦納和奈及利亞，「山藥節」指稱為他們的豐收慶祝活動，故本題答案為 (B) 西非觀光組織。
3. 本文於第二段舉出許多國家慶祝豐收的方式，而最後一段提到儘管依據不同的文化，習俗可能各「不相同」，但在這個特殊的日子，感恩的想法在全球各地都是一樣的，故本題答案為 (B) 有所不同。
4. 根據第一段的敘述，在臺灣，阿美族部落慶祝「豐年祭」；在韓國，他們稱它「秋夕」；在奈及利亞，「山藥節」指稱為他們的豐收慶祝活動。

進階練習　C

解析 由本圖表來看，感恩節大餐的平均花費由 1990 年的 28.85 美元逐漸成長到 2020 年的 49.25 美元，顯示人們過去花費的金額較現在少了許多，故本題答案為 (C) 1990 年的感恩節大餐花費比 2020 年還低。

延伸活動

1. D　2. A　3. E　4. C　5. B

👁 課文中譯

「古老的華人祕方」是 1970 年代的電視商業廣告。你知道這是什麼的商業廣告嗎？是有關藥方的書，還是食譜？其實是洗衣粉廣告！

你可能會疑惑是不是華人以洗衣出名。當然不是！然而，在早期，許多在美國的華裔移民靠洗衣謀生。這就是當談到洗衣粉時，美國人為什麼常會想到華人的原因。聽起來有點可笑，對吧？

事實上，許多商業廣告都包含特定種族或性別的刻板印象。這些商業廣告對某些觀眾而言也許是幽默的，但可能會冒犯，甚至侮辱到其他人。例如，當大家看到一張黑人的臉和他超白的牙齒在取名為 Darkie (黑人) 產品包裝上，他們可能會猜賣的是牙膏。然而，政治和社會趨勢讓大家現在更重視種族和性別平等。自 1980 年代以來，在商業廣告裡，廣告商逐漸使用政治正確的語言。後來，在商業廣告裡，不再有華人銷售古代祕方洗衣粉，而 Darkie 也改名為 Darlie (達莉)。即使如此，部分廣告商仍以刻板印象方式推廣他們的產品。常在商業廣告裡看到女子洗衣，特別是在母親節時促銷洗衣機。而當談到汽車廣告時，你通常會看到男子而非女子開車。

總而言之，下次如果你恰巧在媒體上看到商業廣告，可以留意可能隱藏在背後的刻板印象。你可能會驚訝你所發現的事。

🔺 混合題型

1. B 2. ❸ 3. B 4. D

💡**解析** 1. 由第三段第一句可得知本文的目的在於 (B) 揭露媒體常常以特定種族或性別的刻板印象來作為廣告主軸。

2. 第二段❸提到在早期，許多在美國的華裔移民靠洗衣謀生，故洗衣粉會讓人聯想到華人。

3. 根據第三段第五句和第六句的敘述，自 1980 年代以來，在商業廣告裡，廣告商逐漸使用政治正確的語言，因此，在商業廣告裡，不再有華人銷售古代祕方洗衣粉，而牙膏的品牌名稱也由 Darkie (黑人) 改名為 Darlie (達莉)，故本題答案為 (B)。

4. 第三段第七句提到部分廣告商仍以刻板印象方式推廣他們的產品，由此可知 (D) 歧視的現象仍然會出現在某些廣告中。

✖ 進階練習 B

💡**解析** 由 (C) 和 (D) 圖來看女性仍然在傳統社會中擔任家庭照顧者的角色，符合「男主外，女主內」的刻板印象；而 (A) 圖中的男女可能為上司和下屬的關係，女性對於男性的肢體碰觸感到不舒服，表現出「男女權力不對等」的現象，而本題 (B) 圖顯示男女皆可從軍，且不以顏色框架性別角色，最能突顯出「性別平等」的概念。

✏ 延伸活動 (參考解答)

1. I am good at playing the piano
2. safety cannot be emphasized too much
3. I've been to over thirty countries
4. we think of its nickname, "the Big Apple"

Unit 4 The Culture of Food

飲食文化

課文中譯

食物給我們提供了一個了解世界的重要窗口。世界上不同的地方有截然不同的飲食文化。食物因地而異。你是否曾經疑惑人們為什麼會吃特定種類的食物？

在現今世界，由於有效率的交通工具，長在智利的莓果可以快速空運到德國。新鮮海產可在日本準備，然後僅僅幾小時內就運到臺北一家連鎖餐廳。然而，事情並非總是這樣。在過去，人們靠居住地可獲得的食物為生。換句話說，環境對他們食物的選擇影響很大。

例如，早期臺灣的客家人吃客家食物，以便承受得住他們艱困的生活條件。大多數客家人過去經常進行大量體力勞動，也因此偏好較濃烈的口味。此外，他們必須多日翻山越嶺運送貨物。為了讓食品保存更久，客家人善於風乾、鹽漬或醃製食品。然而，幾世紀以來，秘魯人主要食用馬鈴薯。這些根莖類蔬菜在這裡種植容易，且幫助人們熬過寒冷乾燥的氣候。多年來，他們已經種出逾三千種不同種類馬鈴薯。如今，秘魯是馬鈴薯的最大出口國之一。

影響我們食物選擇的因素不只是我們的喜好，更是我們能從環境中取得什麼。從不同地區的不同食物，人們可以發現每一種飲食文化都很獨特。

混合題型

1. A　2. B　3. C　4. ❻

解析 1. 作者於第一段最後一句提出問題「你是否曾經疑惑人們為什麼會吃特定種類的食物？」，故本題答案為 (A)。

2. 第一段第一句提到食物給我們提供了一個了解世界的重要「窗口」，此處的窗口是指 (B) 學習事物的管道。

3. 第二段第一句提到長在智利的莓果可以快速空運到德國，而同段第二句「新鮮海產可在日本準備，然後僅僅幾小時內就運到臺北一家連鎖餐廳」的目的在於 (C) 證明交通工具的確改變了我們的飲食。

4. 第三段❻提到馬鈴薯這種根莖類蔬菜在秘魯這裡種植容易，而且可以幫助人們熬過寒冷乾燥的氣候。

進階練習　C

解析 (A) 圖顯示現代人經常使用手機來尋找所有和飲食相關的資訊；(B) 圖中的人正在速食或蔬食兩種飲食方式之間作抉擇；(C) 圖顯示俄羅斯和美國兩種不同的飲食文化；(D) 圖顯示訂單處理流程概念圖，消費者選擇商品、結帳付款並經過業者作業時間後，再透過物流服務將商品送給消費者。本文強調世界上不同的地方有不同的食物和文化，故本題答案為 (C)。

延伸活動

1. F　2. I　3. G　4. H　5. J　6. C　7. D　8. A　9. B　10. E

👁 課文中譯

　　當你到世界各地觀光或出差，最好了解在地習俗。否則會有所誤解。例如，事情進展順利時，美國和臺灣的人都會豎起大拇指。然而，如果你在澳洲、中東以及西非的某些國家這樣做，是在侮辱人。在臺灣，如果有人將拇指和食指連結成圈圈，意思是「沒問題」。與此相反，這對巴西人和希臘人來說是侮辱的。

　　同樣的手勢在世界各地的意思可能大不相同。因此，弄清楚這些手勢在你造訪的國家代表什麼意義是很重要的。這可以幫你不惹上麻煩。如果你試圖初次和人見面時就留下好印象，你必須知道如何打招呼。當你在日本時，要向人鞠躬。在西方國家，握手和親吻雙頰通常是可接受的。

　　那飲食習慣是如何呢？在東亞，人們用筷子吃飯，西方則用刀叉。在印度，人們只用右手進食。他們將食物混在一起，揉成小球，再以手指將它們送進嘴裡。然而，左手不應該在吃飯時使用，因為印度人通常在上洗手間時用這隻手。因此，在印度，用左手進食絕對是禁忌。

　　俗話說：「入境隨俗」。這句諺語對你的幫助可能超過你的想像。

🔺 混合題型

1. C　2. D　3. ❺　4. D

💡**解析** 1. 第一段第一句即點出當你到世界各地觀光或出差，最好了解在地習俗。否則會有所誤解。接著，比較不同國家對於豎起大拇指以及將拇指和食指連結成圈圈這兩種手勢的解讀，故本題答案為 (C)。

2. 根據第二段第五句的敘述，當你在日本初次和人見面時，要向人鞠躬，故本題答案為 (D)。

3. 第三段❺提到左手不應該在吃飯時使用，因為印度人通常在上洗手間時用這隻手。

4. 本文主旨在於闡述各國的文化禁忌和風俗習慣，建議出國旅行者最好先對在地習俗有一些認識，以免有所誤解，故最有可能出現在 (D)。

✂ 進階練習　B

💡**解析** 由情境 A 和 B 圖來看，圖片中的瑪麗和約翰做了豎起大拇指以及將拇指和食指連結成圈圈的兩種手勢，不過情境 A 和 B 的人們卻有著截然不同的反應。根據本文第一段的敘述，不同國家的人對於同一手勢的解讀有所不同，故本題答案為 (B)。

📐 延伸活動

1. A　2. D　3. B　4. E　5. C

課文中譯

你看過皮卡丘、蜘蛛人或其他動畫人物走在街上嗎？如果有的話，他們可能是角色扮演玩家。角色扮演是「服裝」和「扮演」的混合字。一開始是打扮成動畫、漫畫、電子遊戲、科幻電影裡的角色。

在 1980 年代，角色扮演首先獲得日本動畫迷的關注。這些粉絲聚在一起、分享想法，並打扮成自己喜歡的角色。當角色扮演玩家的人數增加，更多角色扮演活動就開始舉行。1990 年代，角色扮演的浪潮風行亞洲國家和西方。如今，角色扮演的盛會每年在不同國家舉行，吸引成千上萬名粉絲。

一些角色扮演玩家對設計和創作漂亮有趣的服裝感興趣。其他人專注於表演。這些玩家研究他們選擇的角色，嘗試「變成」他們。因此，有多場比賽會舉行。它們選拔最佳服裝、最佳玩家等。此外，人們也盡情裝扮成同性和異性的角色。

許多人初次看到角色扮演玩家，可能覺得他們有點傻、奇怪或很幼稚。然而，顯而易見的，角色扮演是充滿樂趣的嗜好。這給人們一個平臺，利用想像力盡情地玩。所以，如果玩角色扮演，你會選擇扮演哪個角色呢？

混合題型

1. B　2. C　3. ❹　4. C

解析 1. 本文主旨在於介紹角色扮演的起源和角色扮演玩家如何享受角色扮演的樂趣，故本題答案為 (B)。

2. 根據本文第二段的敘述，在 1980 年代，角色扮演首先獲得日本動畫迷的關注，而後於 1990 年代，角色扮演的浪潮風行亞洲國家和西方，成為一個有趣的文化現象，故最有可能出現在 (C) 文化專欄。

3. 第一段❹提到角色扮演家所打扮的角色來自於動畫、漫畫、電子遊戲、科幻電影裡的角色。

4. 根據第三段最後一句的敘述，角色扮演玩家盡情裝扮成同性和異性的角色，故本題答案為 (C) 男人可以裝扮成女性角色。

進階練習　D

解析 根據本文第二段的敘述，在 1980 年代，角色扮演首先獲得日本動畫迷的關注，而後於 1990 年代，角色扮演的浪潮風行亞洲國家和西方，故最符合第二段的圖片應為 (D) 圖。

延伸活動

1. character　　2. opposite　　3. contest　　4. imagination
A. childish　　B. evident　　C. cosplay　　D. hobby

Unit 7 — My Nights with Lara

我和蘿拉相伴的夜晚

課文中譯

　　過去三個月我睡得不好。晚上我只睡幾小時，清晨就醒。我女兒蘿拉是我夜裡失眠的原因。新生兒很少睡一整夜。自從蘿拉三個月前出生以後，我每晚都要醒好幾次。

　　你是否疑惑，我和蘿拉相伴的夜晚，我的妻子在哪裡？我的妻子在睡覺。隔天她必須上班。在挪威，多年來，父母可請越來越多的帶薪育嬰假。有特定的假保留給父親，不能轉移給母親。然後父母才分配剩餘的育嬰假。

　　育嬰假的法律規範各國不同。在臺灣，小孩滿三歲之前，父母雙方都可以申請最多兩年的育嬰假。此外，在前六個月，他們每月可以領取六成月薪的津貼。然而，在美國，大多數勞工沒有休育嬰假的權利。

　　我有些朋友仍然認為，在家照顧小孩是母親的職責。然而，我認為父母雙方都該承擔責任，了解新生兒。我不願意拿任何東西來交換我和蘿拉相伴而失眠的夜晚。

混合題型

1. ❺　2. D　3. C　4. A

解析 1. 第一段❺提到蘿拉三個月前出生，由此可知她是三個月大的小女嬰。
2. 第三段第一句提到育嬰假的法律規範各國不同，並提出臺灣和美國的例子，故本題答案為 (D)。
3. 第二段第四句提到挪威對於育嬰假的法律規範，而第三段第二句和最後一句分別提到臺灣和美國對於育嬰假的做法，只有瑞典未在文中出現，故本題答案為 (C)。
4. 根據第四段最後兩句的敘述，作者認為父母雙方都該承擔責任，了解新生兒。作者不願意拿任何東西來交換他和蘿拉相伴而失眠的夜晚。由此可知 (A) 作者樂於休育嬰假。

進階練習　B

解析 由本圖表來看，D 國的帶薪育嬰假最長，而 B 國人民的帶薪育嬰假天數比 A 國還長，故本題答案為 (B) C 國人民可以申請二十六週的帶薪育嬰假。

延伸活動

1. It's a firefighter's mission to put the fire out
2. It's every passenger's responsibility to fasten his or her seat belt
3. It's each family member's duty to do the household chores

👁 課文中譯

大部分父母擔憂他們孩子的教育是在預料之中。結果,這種擔憂常常轉變成「更多」——更多課程、更多考試、更多家庭作業和孩子身上更多的壓力。

然而,芬蘭人採取了不同的方法——「少就是多」哲學。一般來說,芬蘭學生花在正規教育上的時間比較少,花在獲取其他類型知識的時間比較多。在芬蘭,學生實際花在學校的時間也較少。典型的上學日從上午九點開始,到下午兩點左右結束。這讓學生有更多時間放鬆和發展自己的興趣。此外,教師可以有更多時間備課,並幫助需要額外協助的學生。因為他們相信學業表現並非全部,因此芬蘭人的考試比較少也就不足為奇了。儘管學生考試和家庭作業比較少,他們仍然得到完善的教育,甚至學業表現突出。

這種做法行得通嗎?結果出奇的好。根據多項研究,芬蘭除了擁有一些世上最頂尖的學生之外,還有一些最快樂的學生。因此,當談到教育時,很明顯的,少其實可能更多。

△ 混合題型

1. C 2. B 3. C 4. ❼

💡 **解析** 1. 作者於第一段大部分父母因為擔憂孩子的教育,往往會給更多的課程、考試和家庭作業,但這也同時造成孩子有更多壓力;第二段引出芬蘭人採取了不同的方法——「少就是多」哲學作為對照,故本題答案為 (C) 另一種學習的做法。

2. 作者於第三段第三句和第四句提到芬蘭除了擁有一些世上最頂尖的學生之外,還有一些最快樂的學生,也提及當談到教育時,少其實可能更多,由此可知作者對於「少就是多」哲學抱持著 (B) 肯定的態度。

3. 第三段第二句提到芬蘭的教育成果出奇的好,由此可知 (C) 芬蘭人的教育做法或許值得學習。

4. 第二段❼提到芬蘭人的考試比較少是因為他們相信學業表現並非全部。

✏ 進階練習 A

💡 **解析** 本文主旨在於介紹芬蘭人的「少就是多」哲學,強調芬蘭學生的在校時間、考試和家庭作業比較少,但是仍然得到完善的教育,甚至學業表現突出,擁有一些世上最頂尖的學生和最快樂的學生,故最符合本文主旨的圖片應為 (A) 圖。

🖼 延伸活動

1. 9:00–9:45   2. History   3. Finnish   4. PE

👁 課文中譯

　　愛情和婚姻今昔大不同。過去，未來夫婿或妻子通常由家裡的人決定。年輕人被期待早婚。直到結婚前，男女通常不准單獨相處。他們見面時，一位監護人會跟著。監護人通常是年長婦人，她的工作是確保年輕男女表現得體。所以，年輕男女只能彼此聊天，接吻或牽手是不被允許的。那時候，約會行為的規矩相當嚴格。

　　相比之下，我們今天的社會就不一樣了。大家通常晚婚或獨立生活。家庭對單身人士的影響沒有那麼大。三十多歲的人大部分太獨立以致於父母無法掌控。然而，其中有一些人還是會尋求親朋好友的意見。他們會接受安排去相親。

　　如今，越來越多人運用科技來幫助他們尋找真愛。線上約會變得更加流行。大家用線上約會網站和智慧型手機的線上約會應用程式尋找伴侶。他們會先建立個人簡介，展現他們的最佳特質。有了這些有效率的方法，他們可以找到更多合適的候選人出來約會。然而，只有時間能判斷這些方法能否帶來長久的關係。

🔺 混合題型

1. A　2. A　3. C　4. ❻

💡**解析** 1. 第一段第一句即點出愛情和婚姻今昔大不同，隨後於同段提到，在過去，婚姻通常由家裡的人決定、男女通常不准單獨相處等嚴格的規範，而後在第二段提到現代人通常晚婚或獨立生活，家庭的影響沒有那麼大，故本文的結構是 (A) 依照時間先後順序來敘述論點。

2. 本文主旨在於比較愛情和婚姻從傳統到現代社會的演變，由過去的男女授受不親到如今網路交友的風氣日盛，故本題答案為 (A)。

3. 第一段第四句、第五句和第六句提到未婚男女不可單獨見面，須有監護人陪同；而監護人通常是年長婦人，她的工作是確保年輕男女表現得體，故本題答案為 (C)。

4. 作者於第三段❻指出只有時間能證明線上約會網站和智慧型手機的線上約會應用程式能否帶來長久的關係，由此可以推測作者對於這些方法的實用性抱持著懷疑的態度。

✏ 進階練習　Billy

💡**解析** 凱莉在自我介紹中提到自己想要找的對象是充滿創意和點子的人，而且她本身也是貓咪愛好者，因此和她最速配的對象應該是會到貓咪收容所當志工的點子王——比利。

📑 延伸活動

1. Online dating is becoming more popular
2. My parents are becoming old
3. The leaves are turning red in the park / The leaves in the park are turning red

The Greatest Inventions of All Time

史上最偉大的發明

👁 課文中譯

我們的世界由許多傑出的發明形塑而成。電燈泡讓我們得以輕鬆在夜裡工作，並有社交生活。現代交通工具，像是汽車、火車和飛機，讓我們能快速地長距離移動。印刷機讓訊息在眾人之間廣泛散布。電子產品，像是廣播和電視，讓我們得以接收和傳遞全球訊息。新技術，像是網際網路和智慧型手機，讓我們即時與世界各地的人交流。哪些發明對你來說最重要，又有哪些是你生活不需要的呢？

想像一個沒有這些出色發明的世界。沒有汽車或其他有效率的交通方式，我們就必須住在很靠近辦公室的地方。如果家人住得很遠，我們也許每隔幾年才能去探望一次。旅行會是負擔不起的奢侈品。我們不會有機會探索世界，學習不同的文化。沒有印刷機，訊息無法迅速散布。沒有網際網路或甚至電話，溝通會很困難，因為可能要花上好幾週才能把信件遞送到。我們對世界的了解會受限。我們的世界觀會很薄弱。

人類創造許多成功的發明。過去幾個世代，偉大的發明改變了我們的生活以及看待世界的方式。少了這一些了不起的發明，我們不會那麼見多識廣，也不會那麼有聯繫，而變得比較孤立。我們應該從過去學習並放眼未來。你覺得我們需要何種新發明以開創更美好的未來呢？

🔷 混合題型

1. C　2. C　3. A　4.

	advantage(s)
light bulbs	allow us to easily work and have a social life at night
airplanes	allow us to travel great distances fast
television	allow us to receive and pass on information globally
smartphones	allow us to communicate with people immediately all over the world

💡**解析** 1. 本文第一段先提出許多傑出的發明以及它們如何形塑了我們現在的生活，第二段提到如果沒有這些發明，我們的生活將會產生哪些重大的變化，故本文的結構是 (C) 依照比較和對照的結構來敘述論點。
　　　2. 本文以提出問題的方式來結束第一段，其目的在於 (C) 引起讀者的興趣，並且使讀者反思如果沒有這些發明，生活會有多麼不便。
　　　3. 根據第三段最後一句的敘述，作者希望讀者思考能夠為人類開創更美好未來的新發明，故本題答案為 (A)。
　　　4. 第一段第二句提到電燈泡讓我們得以輕鬆在夜裡工作，並有「社交生活」；同段第五句提到電視讓我們得以「接收和傳遞」全球訊息；同段第六句提到智慧型手機讓我們即時與世界各地的人「交流」。

✂ 進階練習　　D

💡**解析** 本文主旨在於介紹各種科學發明以及它們對於人類的貢獻，故最有可能出現在 (D) 以科學博覽會為主題的雜誌刊物中。

📐 延伸活動

2. car	3. train	4. airplane	5. printing	6. radio
7. television	8. telephone	9. Internet	10. smartphone	11. invention

課文中譯

　　在嬰兒出生前幾個月，我們就知道它的性別了。有些父母甚至會辦性別揭露派對。親朋好友都圍在一個特別的蛋糕旁。然後，他們切一塊出來揭密——藍色蛋糕內層代表男孩，粉紅色就代表女孩。然而，是男孩或女孩的真正意義何在？越來越多人開始質疑，究竟是否有必要辨認明確的性別。

　　傳統上，大家都稱讚男孩力量大。不論是和朋友上足球場或待在家裡，男孩都被認為精力旺盛。另一方面，女孩被期待願意跟彼此講出內心感受。她們可能以較情緒性的方式，而非冷靜與人互動。從很小開始，男孩就被教導不能哭，而女孩哭則沒關係。

　　這些性別刻板印象造成的弊大於利。不論你把各種特質認定為剛或柔，所有人都是有柔有剛。現實情況是，一個小男孩可以喜歡踢足球，也可以願意花時間在廚房包餃子。一個小女孩可以喜歡玩洋娃娃，也同時愛解數學題。只有當社會不再給人必須以某些方式行事的壓力，大家才能享受做自己的真樂趣。

混合題型

1. B　2. C　3. ❺　4. D

> 解析 1. 本文第二段先闡述一般人對於男女性別的刻板印象，而後於第三段提出其實所有人都是有柔有剛，社會應該停止以性別的刻板印象來施壓於個人，大家才能享受做自己的真樂趣，因此本文最有可能出現在 (B) 探討性別平等的網站中。
>
> 　　2. 第二段最後一句提到男孩從小就被教導不能哭，「而」女孩哭則沒關係，故本題答案為 (C) 對照之意。
>
> 　　3. 第三段❺提到只有當社會不再以性別的刻板印象來約束個人的行為舉止，每個人才能享受做自己的真樂趣。
>
> 　　4. 根據第三段第二句的敘述可得知所有人都是有柔有剛，無法以性別來判斷其個性，故本題答案為 (D)。

進階練習　D

> 解析 根據第三段第二句、第三句和第四句的敘述，所有人都是有柔有剛，因此小男孩可以喜歡踢足球，也喜歡下廚做菜，而小女孩可以喜歡玩洋娃娃，也愛解數學題，故最符合本文主旨的圖片應為 (D) 圖。

延伸活動

2.
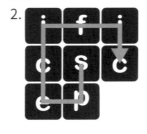

3.
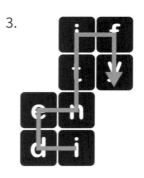

4.
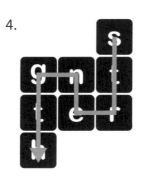

你適合做蘇活族嗎？

👁 課文中譯

你想要在家賺錢嗎？工作時想怎麼穿就怎麼穿嗎？喜歡彈性的工作時段？可以接受不穩定的收入？討厭有老闆？如果所有的這些問題，你都回答「是」，你就是適合當蘇活族，代表在小型辦公室或在家工作的人。

由於數位科技的迅速發展，幾乎人人都可以靠當蘇活族謀生！一些備受歡迎的選擇是自由業者、網路名人、網站設計師或線上賣家。想像如果不必離家就能賺錢且工作時沒老闆在旁邊，會有多美妙！這一定是許多人夢寐以求的工作。

儘管蘇活族享有一般員工沒有的多項優勢，但當蘇活族其實不如外表光鮮。首先，你可能好幾個月都沒有任何收入！其次，你必須一直想出新點子、服務或產品，才能獲利。除此之外，因為缺乏一家公司可以提供的資助和資源，你必須比普通辦公室裡的其他任何人工作得更努力。最後，由於老闆沒有在旁邊，你在工作上必須非常勤勞且要管理規劃讓工作如期完成。

成為蘇活族可以有很多樂趣。然而，能否成功取決於你的性格及自律。所以，你準備好當蘇活族了嗎？

🔺 混合題型

1. C　2. ❶　3. A　4. A

💡**解析** 1. 本文主旨在於介紹一種在小型辦公室辦公或是居家辦公的工作類型，並且提出數個當蘇活族的優缺點以及作為一個成功的蘇活族的必要條件，故本題答案為 (C)。

2. 第二段❶提到數位科技的迅速發展是促成人們能夠居家辦公當蘇活族的主因。

3. 第三段第四句提到蘇活族缺乏公司的資助和資源，所以必須更努力工作，此句承接上句蘇活族「必須一直想出新點子、服務或產品，才能獲利」的語意，故本題答案為 (A) 除此之外。

4. 根據本文第三段的敘述，作為一個蘇活族必須時時創新、勤勞工作，而且還得自我管理才能如期完成客戶的託付，故本題中的 (A) 山姆・史密斯是可靠的、有創意的和負責的人，最有可能是蘇活族。

✖ 進階練習　C

💡**解析** 由本圖表來看，蘇活族以橘色線 (年滿二十五歲以上且具有碩博士學歷者) 和淺藍色線 (年滿二十五歲以上且具有學士學歷者) 的比例較高，由此可知 (C) 年滿二十五歲以上者的教育水平越高，其選擇居家辦公的比例也會越高。

📐 延伸活動

1. F　2. C　3. B　4. H　5. G　6. J　7. D　8. E　9. A　10. I

課文中譯

十月最後一個星期六，許多人在臺北遊行，一路歡呼並揮舞彩虹旗。這是臺灣同志驕傲遊行的典型場景 (女同志、男同志、雙性戀、跨性別人士、酷兒、雙性人和無性戀者)，這遊行自 2003 年開始，此後每年舉辦一次。第一次活動不太大，僅約兩千人參加遊行。然而，這些年來，越來越多人，不論他們的性別為何，願意走上街頭支持這項活動。

這一切始於 1969 年紐約的一個夜晚。那晚，警察來到一家名為石牆的同志酒吧，並開始無故逮人。酒吧裡的人對警察很憤怒，爆發鬥毆衝突。隨後，那家酒吧被許多憤怒的女同志及男同志團體成員包圍。為了自身安全，警察被迫躲在酒吧內。衝突拉鋸多天才落幕。隔年，舉行了首場同志驕傲遊行以紀念此一重要事件。石牆酒吧的鬥爭激勵眾人拒絕來自政府的惡劣對待，且勇敢維護自己的權利。

後來，各式各樣的同志驕傲示威遊行開始在全球各地的許多大城市，例如紐約、赫爾辛基和伯明罕，每年舉辦。至今，包含臺灣在內的許多國家，已讓同性婚姻合法化。同志權利在全球各地逐漸獲得重視、受到尊重。

混合題型

1. C　2. C　3. B　4. ❼

解析 1. 本文主旨在於介紹同志驕傲遊行的起源和其訴求，故最符合本文主旨的圖片應為 (C) 圖。

2. 根據第三段第一句的敘述，同志驕傲示威遊行每年都會在全球各地的許多大城市舉辦，例如紐約、赫爾辛基和伯明罕，故本題答案為 (C)。

3. 本文以同志驕傲遊行、同性婚姻合法化和同志權利為主軸，故最適合本文的口號為 (B) 愛不分性別。

4. 第二段❼提到首場同志驕傲遊行的舉辦是為了要紀念石牆同志酒吧的衝突事件。

進階練習　D

解析 LGBTQIA 由女同志、男同志、雙性戀、跨性別人士、酷兒、雙性人和無性戀者等英文字的第一個字母縮寫而成，而 BBC 也是使用英國、廣播和公司等英文字的第一個字母縮寫而成，故本題答案為 (D)。

延伸活動

1. A　2. D　3. B　4. C　5. E

課文中譯

　　你覺得完美假期是什麼樣子的呢？對某些人來說，令人愉快的出遊可能是在美麗的海灘待上一週。其他人可能喜歡週末入住奢華旅館。對許多年輕人而言，最佳旅行可能是一趟世界各個角落的個人旅行。

　　以前，許多人透過旅行社預訂行程，並且跟著導遊走。這種旅行方式稱為「套裝旅行」。他們付錢給旅行社代辦瑣事，像是交通，然後一切都安排好了。然而，自 1960 年代開始，年輕的旅行者決定換個方式行事。他們扔掉厚重的行李和導遊。此外，他們全靠自己做好安排，盡可能少帶東西旅行。

　　這些旅行者被稱為背包客，背著背包旅行的人。他們搭大眾交通工具、住青年旅社，並且吃當地的食物。他們的目標是只花很少的錢去看世界。他們想要旅行更久，以便於更加了解自己和他們造訪的國家。

　　隨後的幾年間，背包客在世界各地遊歷。有些人免費搭便車旅行，有些人騎腳踏車，有些人甚至徒步四處走。如今，年輕人的旅行方式已經從背包旅行逐漸演變到沙發衝浪。旅行者不住旅館或青年旅社，而是睡在當地人家中的沙發上。他們認為這是體驗當地文化和探索世界最好的方式。

混合題型

1. B　2. ❶　3. A　4. A

解析 1. 根據第四段第三句的敘述，如今，年輕人的旅行方式已經從背包旅行逐漸演變到沙發衝浪，故本題 (B) 圖所提供的資訊是背包客最需要的。

2. 第三段 ❶ 提到背包客就是指背著背包旅行的人。

3. (B) 在第四段最後一句提到年輕人認為沙發衝浪是體驗當地文化和探索世界最好的方式；(C) 在第二段第四句、第五句和第六句提到 1960 年代開始興起一種有別於以往有導遊帶領、有旅行社打點好一切事宜的旅行方式；(D) 在第三段第四句提到年輕人喜歡當背包客是因為他們想要更長期旅行，利用旅行來了解自己和他們造訪的國家。故本題只有 (A) 獨自旅行的危險未在本文中出現。

4. 作者只有在本文中提到當背包客的旅行方式以及年輕人偏好當背包客的原因，並未針對背包旅行提出任何個人的觀點和看法，由此可以推測作者對於背包旅行抱持著 (A) 中立的態度。

✎ 進階練習

Characteristics	Package tour	Backpacking
1. Hire a tour guide.	✓	
2. Find a tour agency.	✓	
3. Use public transportation more.		✓
4. Book train tickets by themselves.		✓
5. Explore the world on foot.		✓
6. Have only a few necessary items in carry-on bags.		✓
7. Travel by getting free rides.		✓
8. Sleep at the local's house without paying.		✓
9. Stay in a luxury hotel more.	✓	
10. Travel with heavy baggage.	✓	

💡**解析** 根據第二段第一句、第二句和第三句的敘述，套裝旅行是由導遊領隊，且旅行社會代辦瑣事，像是交通等旅行相關事宜。此外，由第二段第四句和第五句可以推測不同於背包客，參加套裝旅行的旅客大多攜帶厚重的行李出遊。第二段最後一句、第三段和第四段提到背包客喜歡自己安排行程，而且盡可能地輕裝出發，他們會搭大眾交通工具、搭便車或是徒步四處走，並且睡在當地人家中的沙發來節省花費。

📖 延伸活動 (參考解答)

hotel	travel	hostel	baggage
hostel	baggage	**travel**	hotel
travel	hotel	baggage	**hostel**
baggage	**hostel**	hotel	travel

16

How Voice Recognition Technology Changes Our Lives

語音辨識技術如何改變我們的生活

👁 課文中譯

你是否曾想過電腦將來會變成什麼樣子？我們還會在電腦螢幕上看圖片或影片嗎？我們還需要打字嗎？透過語音辨識技術，鍵盤最終變得不需要了。

使用語音辨識技術，或稱 VRT，是一種動態的過程，過程中電腦可將多種口語轉化為文字。一些電子設備，像是智慧型手機已配備 VRT。總體而言，準確性很不錯，但部分設備仍難以辨別發音相似的名稱和字彙。VRT 開發人員面臨的另一個問題是口音。兩個人講同一種語言聽起來差異可能很大，取決於他們成長的區域。然而，隨時間累積，研發人員會逐步克服這些阻礙，不久後，VRT 就將能理解任何一種口音。

語音辨識技術不僅適用於電子裝置，也還能用在我們的房子。當你站在房門口，可以只說「開燈」，房間就會亮燈。不必用遙控器，你可以說，「打開電視，轉到電影頻道」。然後，就能享受看電影的樂趣。總而言之，VRT 的可能性是無限的，它允許你盡情發揮想像力。

混合題型

1. B　2. (1) false (2) true (3) not given (4) false (5) true　3. A　4. ❺

💡**解析** 1. 本文主旨在於介紹語音辨識技術、該技術目前面臨的問題和可應用的範疇，故本題答案為 (B) 口語命令可被執行。

2. 根據第二段第三句和第四句的敘述，VRT 仍難以辨別發音相似的名稱和字彙，且另一個問題是口音，其準確性仍然有問題；第三段最後一句提到 VRT 允許你盡情發揮想像力；第二段第二句僅提到智慧型手機已配備 VRT，但是並未提及它會讓手機使用者比較不聰明；根據第二段第一句的敘述，VRT 可將多種口語轉化為文字，由此可知不僅限於英文；第三段第三句提到 VRT 讓使用者不必用遙控器就可以打開電視並且選擇頻道。

3. 本文和語音辨識技術有關，因此最有可能出現在 (A) 科學期刊中。

4. 作者於第三段❺提到 VRT 的可能性是無限的，它允許你盡情發揮想像力，由此可以推測作者對於 VRT 抱持著正向肯定的態度。

進階練習　D

💡**解析** (A) 圖提到可以使用 VRT 來調控溫度；(B) 圖中的電視可以使用 VRT 來打開或關閉電源並且切換頻道；(C) 圖中的電玩強調使用者可以用身體動作和聲音來操控遊戲進行；(D) 圖的智慧型手機只有提到有觸控式螢幕，並沒有提及 VRT，故本題答案為 (D) 圖。

延伸活動 (參考解答)

1. (1) Turn on the light. / Turn the light on. / Switch on the light.
   (2) Turn off the light. / Turn the light off. / Switch off the light.
2. (1) Turn up the volume. / Turn the volume up. / Increase the volume.
   (2) Turn down the volume. / Turn the volume down. / Decrease the volume.
3. (1) Open the door.　(2) Lock the door.

👁 課文中譯

此時此刻，你在社群媒體追蹤誰？他或她是正在狼吞虎嚥的大胃王、開箱最新款智慧型手機的科技迷，還是在卸妝的模特兒？任何你在社群媒體追蹤的人都被稱為網路名人或是社群媒體影響者。透過網路直播自己想要的任何主題，他或她可以有「不錯」的收入，因為現在什麼都可以拿來賺錢！

第一個網路直播由蘋果公司於 1995 年推出，以娛樂為目的，是紐約夜店演唱會的聲音直播。後來，搖滾樂團使用此方式在網路上放送實況演唱會。至今，在世界各地，幾乎人人可以在任何時間做任何主題的網路直播。任何擁有智慧型手機或電腦的人，都可以在線上分享他或她任何感興趣的主題。

網路直播也成為商業很重要的一部分。有些公司網路直播會談、會議和教育訓練的影片。其他公司利用這項技術進行銷售和行銷。此外，教育也大受網路直播所影響。學生不必進教室就能上課。這有助於鼓勵自學或甚至終身學習。此外，網路直播還左右了選舉，甚至是選民的決定。許多從政者有社群媒體帳戶，會定期製作網路直播，分享他們的政策或甚至生活。藉由和觀眾互動，他們想搏取選民的信任並贏得選舉。

顯然，網路直播起初是一種娛樂形式，現在已經影響了我們的行事方法、學習途徑，甚至思考方式。因此，小心不要被數百萬的網路直播主愚弄了！

🔺 混合題型

1. D　2. B　3. ❷　4. D

💡**解析** 1. 第二段第二句提到搖滾樂團使用直播的方式在網路上放送他們的「實況」演唱會，故本題答案為 (D)。

2. 本文第三段的主旨在於闡述各種直播的應用範疇以及其接受對象，例如：學校教學或政見宣傳等，故本題答案為 (B) 直播如何影響到我們的生活。

3. 圖中的職員們正在觀看多方視訊會議的過程，因此最符合第三段❷中所提到「有些公司網路直播會談、會議和教育訓練的影片」的敘述。

4. 根據第二段最後一句的敘述，世界上任何擁有智慧型手機或電腦的人，都可以在線上分享他或她任何感興趣的主題，故本題以 (D) 圖中使用智慧型手機且有「實況」和「串流」等字樣最為貼近本文主題。

✂ 進階練習　C

💡**解析** 比較 2010 年和現在的圓餅圖可得知，使用雲端數位學習的比例從百分之五提升至百分之五十。現今，雲端數位學習和面對面學習的比例相同，故本題答案為 (C)。

📐 延伸活動 (參考解答)

1. Whoever　　2. whatever　　3. wherever / whenever　　4. whoever / whomever
5. Whenever　　6. whenever　　7. whoever / whomever　　8. whichever / whatever
9. However　　10. however

👁 課文中譯

　　如果你曾經在電視上看過任何犯罪影片或謀殺懸疑劇，你可能已經注意到警察總是在犯罪現場搜查證據。破解罪犯身分的最重要線索之一就是留在現場的指紋。然而，人們最初是如何開始找指紋並且引證呢？以下是首椿靠指紋破案的故事。

　　這一切始於 1892 年的阿根廷。某一天，兩個孩子在自己家裡被殘暴殺害。當時有兩位嫌疑犯。一位是孩子的母親法蘭西斯卡·羅哈，另一位是他們的鄰居佩卓·雷蒙·維拉斯奎茲。兩位均否認犯罪。幾天後，一位警官愛德華多·阿爾瓦雷茨，被派去協助調查。他在臥室裡發現了一枚血指紋。阿爾瓦雷茨沒有抹掉它，而是決定蒐集這個證據，和兩位嫌疑犯的指紋比對是否一致。警方聯繫了正在研究指紋分類的胡安·布塞蒂奇，以便辨識這些指紋。最後，羅哈被證實有罪。她坦承有位約會對象想娶她，但他不喜歡她的孩子。因此，她選擇奪走孩子的性命。

　　指紋辨識法證實是很有效的，以致於全球各地警察此後持續使用。隨著技術發展，警探現在可以準確地配對指紋，並立即找到罪犯。

△▽ 混合題型

1. A　　2. D　　3. B　　4. ⓫

💡**解析** 1. 作者於第一段第三句提出一個問題「然而，人們最初是如何開始找指紋並且引證呢？」，故本題答案為 (A)。
　　　　 2. 第二段第二句提到有兩個孩子在家裡被殺害，而第四句和第五句提到孩子的母親和鄰居都否認犯罪，由此可以推斷第三句的 suspect 所指的是 (D) 被認為有可能犯罪的人。
　　　　 3. 根據第三段的敘述，故事發生的先後順序為 b. 某一天，兩個孩子在自己家裡被殘暴殺害；d. 孩子的母親和鄰居都是嫌疑犯，不過兩人都否認犯罪；c. 一位警官在臥室裡發現了一枚血指紋，決定將這枚指紋印和兩位嫌疑犯的指紋進行比對；a. 該名母親被證實有罪。故本題答案為 (B)。
　　　　 4. 第二段 ⓫ 提到這名兇手的動機是約會對象想娶她，但他不喜歡她的孩子。

✖ 進階練習　　A

💡**解析** 根據第一段第一句和第二句的敘述，警方會在犯罪現場採集指紋以辨認出兇手的身分，故本題只有 (A) 圖顯示為門禁管制用的指紋辨識功能在本文中未被提及。

📖 延伸活動

☑ 2. Two young children got brutally murdered at home.
☑ 4. The suspects are Francisca Rojas and Pedro Ramón Velázquez.
☑ 5. Eduardo Alvárez helped carry out this investigation.
☑ 8. Juan Vucetich worked on fingerprint classification.
☑ 10. Francisca Rojas confessed to the murder.

The Unknown Part of "The Road Not Taken"

〈未走之路〉不為人知的部分

👁 課文中譯

　　美國的詩作有悠久傳統。華特‧惠特曼，自由詩之父，最崇尚民主自由。希薇亞‧普拉斯，作為一名詩人，走在時代尖端。她探究男性主宰現象，甚至是死亡。至今，詩人多如同天上繁星。但哪一首詩是有史以來最受歡迎的呢？那會是羅伯特‧佛洛斯特的〈未走之路〉。佛洛斯特是位大師，擅寫與世隔絕、鄉野田間和日常生活。

　　對大部分的人來說，這首詩的主要訊息是人生充滿許多選擇，做出的決定當然會影響往後的路。一旦我們做出決定，就不能回頭。過一陣子，我們可能回過頭來看，在想若是選擇不同，人生會變成什麼樣子。這些解釋全都很有道理。當然我們的人生必須做出抉擇，不用說也知道，這些抉擇會影響我們找工作、住哪裡、愛上誰等。

　　但那是這首詩真正的意義嗎？不是的！結果證明，〈未走之路〉很簡單。雖然很多人想了很多這首詩抽象的意義，但它背後的真實故事如下。佛洛斯特住在英國鄉間時，他常和友人愛德華‧湯瑪斯去健行。然而，湯瑪斯經常懊悔所選擇的健行路線。這給了佛洛斯特靈感寫下〈未走之路〉，關於那些他們可能走過的路。不過，這首詩對許多人造成相當大的影響，被認為是有史以來最高人氣的詩作之一。

⬡ 混合題型

1. A　2. C　3. A　4.

	theme(s) of poems
Walt Whitman	democracy and freedom
Sylvia Plath	male domination and even death
Robert Frost	isolation, countryside, and daily life

💡**解析** 1. 第一段第一句提到美國的詩作有悠久傳統，並舉出自由詩之父華特‧惠特曼和走在時代尖端的詩人希薇亞‧普拉斯兩位美國詩壇上的名人作為例子，故本題答案為 (A)。

　　2. 由於美國的詩作有悠久傳統，故作者用「多如同天上繁星」的比喻來形容 (C) 美國詩壇有許多傑出詩人的現象。

　　3. 根據第三段第三句和第四句的敘述，很多人為〈未走之路〉想了很多意義，但它其實很簡單。由此來看 (A) 這是一首被大家誤解的詩，最為正確。

　　4. 第一段第二句提到華特‧惠特曼的詩崇尚民主自由；同段最後一句提到羅伯特‧佛洛斯特擅寫與世隔絕、鄉野田間和日常生活。

✂ 進階練習　C

💡**解析** 根據第三段第五句的敘述，〈未走之路〉是羅伯特‧佛洛斯特住在英國鄉間時的作品，故本題答案為 (C)。

📐 延伸活動

1. decision　　2. poet　　3. numerous　　4. popular　　5. abstract

6. regret　　7. isolation　　8. countryside　　9. daily　　10. democracy

👁 課文中譯

　　人們說牠看起來像大象、龍、巨蛇般的魚以及許多其他動物。據說這個生物在西元 565 年在蘇格蘭第一次被看到。後來，這個生物在 1930 年間再被看到後被廣泛報導。沒人知道是真有其物或是個謎。牠是尼斯湖水怪，綽號尼希。

　　1933 年七月，一對夫妻聲稱，他們沿著尼斯湖開車時，看到一個巨大的生物在他們車前橫越馬路。他們說牠大約 1.2 公尺高、7.6 公尺長。而且，牠的長脖子很像象鼻。一家地方報紙報導此事，故事迅速傳開。一年後，另一名男子拍下怪物自湖中出現的照片，但後來證明是造假。然而，媒體關注讓世界各地的人都想來看尼希。他們來到這座湖，希望能一瞥這隻神祕的水怪。

　　自 1933 年以來，有很多人說看到尼斯湖水怪。許多人將鹿、海豹、波浪，甚至是圓木誤認成尼希。研究員想利用科技找到任何能證明尼希的證據，但目前僅能找到一些水生動物和超過三千種細菌。雖然大部分科學家相信，尼希根本不存在，有些人仍認為牠可能是一種未被發現的恐龍。蘇格蘭高地的尼斯湖水怪至今仍是未解的神祕傳說。

🔺 混合題型

1. A　2. B　3. C　4. ❺

💡 **解析** 1. 根據第二段第四句和第五句的敘述，一家地方報紙報導尼斯湖中有巨大生物的故事，一年後，另一名男子拍下怪物自湖中出現的照片，但是後來證明是造假的，故本題答案為 (A) 假的。

　　2. 根據第二段第二句和第三句的敘述，尼斯湖水怪「大約 1.2 公尺高、7.6 公尺長。而且，牠的長脖子很像象鼻」，故最符合的圖片應為 (B) 圖。

　　3. 第一段第二句和第三句提到牠在蘇格蘭第一次被看到，在 1930 年間再被看到後被廣泛報導；第二段第二句和第三句提到牠大約 1.2 公尺高、7.6 公尺長，而牠的長脖子很像象鼻，故本題答案為 (C)。

　　4. 作者於第三段❺提到「蘇格蘭高地的尼斯湖水怪至今仍是未解的神祕傳說」，由此可以推測作者對於尼希的存在抱持著中立的態度。

✒ 進階練習　Bb

💡 **解析** 根據第一段第二句、第二段第一句和第三段第五句的敘述，尼斯湖水怪的發現地為蘇格蘭的尼斯湖，故本題答案為 Bb。

📐 延伸活動

1. publicity　2. trunk　3. creature　4. mistake　5. bacteria

The Dying Coral Reefs

垂死的珊瑚礁

👁 課文中譯

　　什麼地方是逾一千五百個物種，像是魚、鯨、鯊、海豚、海龜和許多其他海洋動物的棲息地？從外太空能看見地球上現存的最大有機體之一是什麼？哪個生態系統由兩千九百座個別的活珊瑚礁和九百個島嶼組成？那就是大堡礁，被認為是世界七大自然奇觀之一。

　　大堡礁位於澳洲東北海岸。幾乎是臺灣的十倍大，只比日本小一點。觀光在此盛行，因為珊瑚礁周圍的水清澈到能看見美不勝收的水生動物。每年，大堡礁吸引到數百萬觀光客前來見識世上最美的海洋生物和探索五顏六色的珊瑚礁。觀光業有助於澳洲經濟成長，並教育眾人此一自然奇觀。

　　但大堡礁前途未卜。人類活動，像是走在珊瑚礁上和保留珊瑚碎片當紀念品，正傷害著珊瑚礁。除此之外，氣候變遷形成重大威脅。顯然，氣候緊急狀態出現了。它造成海水跟著變暖，導致珊瑚礁大規模白化。珊瑚礁逐漸褪色、變白，然後因為海洋熱浪而死去。科學家已經警告，如果全球暖化持續下去，不久的將來我們就會失去一個世界自然奇觀。

△▽ 混合題型

1. A　2. ❷　3. C　4. A

💡**解析** 1. 根據第三段第二句、第三句和第六句的敘述，人類活動、氣候變遷和海洋熱浪對大堡礁的生存造成威脅，只有鯨魚和鯊魚未被提及，故本題答案為 (A)。

　　2. 第二段 ❷ 提到大堡礁的面積幾乎是臺灣的十倍大，只比日本小一點。

　　3. 根據第二段第一句的敘述，大堡礁位於澳洲東北海岸，故本題答案為 (C)。

　　4. 作者於第三段最後一句提到「科學家已經警告，如果全球暖化持續下去，不久的將來我們就會失去一個世界自然奇觀」，故本題答案為 (A) 以提出警告的方式來結束本文。

✏ 進階練習　A

💡**解析** 根據第三段第五句和第六句的敘述，海水變暖會導致珊瑚礁大規模白化，然後因為海洋熱浪而死去，由此可知珊瑚礁的數量和海水溫度為負相關。由本圖表來看，自 1950 年到 2020 年的海水平均溫度逐漸升高，可推知珊瑚礁的數量會逐年下降，故本題答案為 (A)。

🏷 延伸活動

1. F　2. A　3. E　4. B　5. D　6. C

Gender Roles of the Animal Kingdom

動物界的性別角色

👁 課文中譯

　　如果你以為性別角色僅存在於人類世界，請再想想。在動物界，雄性和雌性都有牠們自己複雜的問題要處理，所以我們至少不孤單。讓我們先談明顯的特徵——體型。在鳥類和哺乳動物中，雄性平均都比雌性大。這是因為雄性往往必須為食物而戰，而且也要能吸引配偶。

　　通常在動物界，雄性越大，就越容易找到牠們的伴侶。為了贏得配偶，許多物種發現誇大體型的方法。例如，牠們會發出低沉的聲音來表明牠們比實際上的大。假如有雌性上當，會以為自己已經擁有所能找到的最強壯或高大的雄性。雄性獅子、無尾熊和紅鹿都被發現聽起來比牠們的實際體型大，以便吸引雌性。

　　另一方面，當談到養育幼崽，性別在動物界也扮演重要角色。通常，照顧蛋的是母親。然而，皇帝企鵝恰好相反。雌企鵝產蛋之後，會前往海裡覓食。在此同時，全職父親不吃不喝，坐在蛋上將近三個月。因此，做出犧牲來養育孩子的不僅是雌性，雄性在照顧幼崽方面也扮演重要角色。

△▽ 混合題型

1. B　2. ❺　3. A　4. (1) true (2) false (3) not given (4) true (5) true

💡**解析** 1. 本文主旨在於 (B) 動物界的性別角色如何扮演。

　　　　2. 第一段❺提到雄性平均都比雌性大，這是因為雄性往往必須為食物而戰，而且也要能吸引配偶。

　　　　3. 第三段第二句和第三句中以皇帝企鵝為例，點出和其他由雌性孵蛋的動物正好相反，皇帝企鵝由雄性孵蛋，故本題答案為 (A) 舉出只有雌性照顧幼崽的例外。

　　　　4. 根據第二段第五句的敘述，雄性獅子、無尾熊和紅鹿都被發現聲音聽起來比牠們的實際體型大，以便吸引雌性；第一段第五句提到雄性體型較大除了為了獵食，也為了吸引配偶；全文未提及體型較大的雌性紅鹿無法吸引雄性紅鹿的注意；第三段第三句、第四句和第五句提到皇帝企鵝恰好相反。雌企鵝產蛋之後，會前往海裡覓食。雄企鵝會不吃不喝地坐在蛋上將近三個月。

📏 進階練習　C

💡**解析** 本文第三段中提到皇帝企鵝乃是由雄性來擔任孵蛋者的角色，此一敘述恰好和 (C) 雄性海馬的腹部有育兒袋裝卵為同一性質的舉例。

📐 延伸活動

1. penguin　　　2. gender　　　3. male　　　4. complicated
A. female　　　B. exaggerate　　C. animal　　　D. lay

課文中譯

1990 年代，好幾位超級名模裸體出鏡，以便採取行動並發聲。她們很同情為了毛皮而被飼養且被殺害的動物。此外，她們也憎惡那些用毛皮製作名牌服裝的人。因此，這些超級名模說，她們上臺寧願不穿衣，也不願意穿皮草。這項宣傳活動奏效。穿皮草不再酷炫，反而是響應環保或所謂的「環保時尚」變酷了。

如今，拒絕使用毛皮還不夠。設計師要了解用來製作衣服的布料是如何生產的甚至更加重要。棉花是否有機栽植？製衣廠工人是否處於合理的工作環境？產品是依據「公平貿易」原則製作出來也十分重要。許多設計師也因為能將回收材料，像是金屬、紙張和老舊橡膠輪胎，應用到自己的設計上而感到自豪。

雖然許多設計師正在改變作風，仍然有許多大型公司拒絕採用環保做法。「快時尚」鼓勵大家購買更多新衣服，穿上最新時尚，然後立即丟棄。一大堆可以穿的衣服被扔掉，變成垃圾。

「響應環保」越來越受歡迎，但有些人仍然喜愛廉價而時髦的衣服，而非對環境友善的產品。為了地球，希望環保產品很快會變成主流趨勢。

混合題型

1. C 2. ❻ 3. C 4. A

解析 1. 由第一段第一句和最後一句可得知本文的目的在於 (C) 描述響應環保的概念如何影響服裝市場。

2. 作者於第一段❻提到穿皮草不再酷炫，反而是響應環保或所謂的「環保時尚」變酷了，由此可以推測作者對於環保時尚抱持著正向的態度。

3. 根據第二段第三句、第五句和最後一句的敘述，設計師們開始關心和衣服的布料生產有關的議題，像是有機棉花的栽植、產品是否依據「公平貿易」的原則製作和應用回收材料到自己的設計等，故本題只有 (C) 圖標榜設計師流行品牌在本文第二段中未被提及。

4. 第四段第一句提到有些人仍然喜愛廉價而時髦的衣服，而非對環境友善的產品。但是「為了」地球，希望環保產品很快會變成主流趨勢，故本題答案為 (A) 為了…的利益。

✐ 進階練習

Characteristics	Eco-fashion	Fast fashion
1. Contain recycled materials.	✓	
2. Keep up with the latest fashion.		✓
3. Persuade customers to buy more.		✓
4. Encourage people to throw old clothes.		✓
5. Produce cheaper clothes.		✓
6. Use eco-friendly materials.	✓	
7. Create more garbage.		✓

💡**解析** 根據本文第二段的敘述，環保時尚重視依據公平貿易原則生產布料，並且使用回收材料或是響應環保的材質來設計衣服；根據第三段第二句、第三句和第四段第一句的敘述，快時尚製造許多人喜愛的廉價而時髦的衣服，鼓勵大家購買更多新衣服，穿上最新時尚，然後立即丟棄，因而製造了許多垃圾。

✐ 延伸活動

1. It is dangerous for a man to swim alone in the river
2. It is healthy for the elderly to exercise regularly
3. It is not recommended for people to overeat

👁 **課文中譯**

　　湯馬斯‧佛里曼寫了一本書叫《世界是平的》，在書中，他描述各國是如何大大地影響彼此，最終模糊了國與國之間的邊界。因此，身為地球村公民，特別重要的是，我們不僅只是從書本上學習。關鍵是體驗不同的文化，永遠抱持學習的熱情。

　　為了拓展思維，許多學生花時間去看世界。有些人進大學前安排空檔年出國旅行。空檔年讓學生能親身去了解其他文化。像是這樣的經驗是很寶貴的，那些學生可能也變得比沒空檔年的人更成熟。然而，對於那些由高中直接進大學的人來說，他們仍然可以透過寒暑假出國唸書或當交換生得到相當多的經驗。他們也可以有很多的機會學習外語、與來自不同背景的人做朋友，並且與當地人交流。一些人甚至申請寄宿家庭。這能幫助他們理解當地家庭的日常生活細項。

　　不管你將來想做什麼樣的工作，體驗外面的世界都很有幫助。它不僅改善你的語言技巧，也開闊你的眼界。這可以轉化成一份更好的工作、更多的興趣或更充實的人生經驗。

🔺 **混合題型**

1. B　2. A　3. ❽　4. B

💡 **解析** 1. 作者於第一段引用湯馬斯‧佛里曼的《世界是平的》一書，描述各國是如何大大地影響彼此，最終模糊了國與國之間的邊界。鼓勵人們走出書本，不是只從書本上學習就特別重要，關鍵是體驗不同的文化，永遠抱持熱情學習，故本題答案為 (B) 鼓勵人們走出書本、向外探索真實的世界。

2. 根據本文第二段的敘述，有些人進大學前安排空檔年出國旅行，有些人透過寒暑假出國唸書或當交換生來親身體驗不同的文化，故只有 (A) 圖一起低頭玩手機的年輕人不符合文中描述體驗外面世界的方式。

3. 第二段❽提到申請寄宿家庭能幫助理解當地家庭的日常生活細項。

4. 根據第三段第二句敘述，體驗外面的世界不僅改善你的語言技巧，也開闊你的眼界，讓你更容易「藉此找到」好的工作、更多的興趣或擁有更充實的人生經驗，故本題答案為 (B) 讓情況發生。

✎ **進階練習**　D

💡 **解析** 由本圖來看，參加三民空檔年展的人數由 2015 年的一千人逐年成長至 2020 年的兩千人，故本題答案為 (D)。

🗂 **延伸活動**

1. The key to success is not only hard work but also preparation.
   (Not only hard work but also preparation is the key to success.)

2. The fear of the flu has led to not only the panic buying of masks but also a steep drop in business.
   (Not only has the fear of the flu led to the panic buying of masks but also a steep drop in business.)

3. The international book fair not only appealed to those who love to read but also to those who don't.
   (Not only did the international book fair appeal to those who love to read but also to those who don't.)

👁 **課文中譯**

　　想像一下，你可以在兩個不同的班做選擇。在 A 班，你被要求坐在課桌前聽講。在 B 班，老師會給你一些用具，把你和同學們分組，設定計時器，要求你們在接下來的三十分鐘內一起完成一項作業。你可以坐等聽講或加入討論並盡力而為。你會選哪一班？

　　每個班都有自己的優點。在 A 班，以授課為主的班級，學生可以在短時間內獲得大量訊息。他們負責認真聽課。然而，這種學習風格有其限制。例如，學生可能習慣於記憶事實，沒有針對議題進行批判性思考。結果，學生可能可以通過多項選擇題的測驗，但難以回答開放式問題。

　　在 B 班，學生有機會直接接觸材料。他們可以透過課堂討論、實驗和合作學到很多。然而，這種學習風格的一個主要缺點是學生的成績和教室氣氛是高度相關的。如果維持不好班級秩序，學生可能感到學習有困難。

　　兩種方法都能調整以合乎個人需求。如果你困於課堂中，那就加入一個小型的學習小組一起討論。如果實際操作的經驗對你沒有幫助，那就花更多時間仔細的研讀。學習不會有錯誤的方法！

📐 **混合題型**

1. C　2. A　3. B　4.

	advantage(s)	**disadvantage(s)**
class A	1. gain a good deal of information in a short time 2. They are responsible for listening carefully to the lesson.	1. without critically thinking about the issues 2. struggle to answer open questions
class B	1. work with the materials directly 2. learn a great deal through class discussions, experiments and cooperation	students' performance is highly associated with the classroom atmosphere

💡 **解析** 1. 本文的第二段和第三段分別就授課、實作兩種學習方法的優缺點進行陳述，故本題答案為 (C)。

2. 由第四段第一句來看，作者認為這兩種方法都能調整以合乎個人需求，由此可知作者對於這兩種學習風格抱持著 (A) 中立的態度。

3. 第三段第二句提到 B 班的學生可以透過討論、實驗和合作學到很多。由此表來看，以彼得喜愛做實驗、熱衷於團隊合作，並且樂於和同學溝通的特點來看，B 班是最適合彼得的班級，故本題答案為 (B)。

4. 根據第二段第二句的敘述，A 班的學習優勢之一在於學生可以在短時間內獲得「大量訊息」；根據第三段第一句和第二句的敘述，B 班的學習優勢之一在於可以透過「討論、實驗和合作」學到很多；同段第三句也提到這種學習風格的一個主要缺點是學生的成績和「教室氣氛」是高度相關的。

解析 由本圖表來看，過去的學生學習偏重閱讀和寫作，而現今的學生偏好以視覺輔助的方式來學習，故本題答案為 (C) 現在有越來越多的學生喜歡透過影片和圖像的方式來學習。

延伸活動

Lecture-based Classes	Discussion-based Classes
A, C, D	B, E, F

閱讀經典文學時光之旅：英國篇

宋美瑾　編著

閱讀經典文學時光之旅：美國篇

陳彰範　編著

- 各書精選8篇經典英美文學作品，囊括各類議題，如性別平等、人權、海洋教育等。獨家收錄故事背景知識補充，帶領讀者深入領略經典文學之美。
- 附精闢賞析、文章中譯及電子朗讀音檔，自學也能輕鬆讀懂文學作品。
- 可搭配新課綱加深加廣選修課程「英文閱讀與寫作」及多元選修課程。

第一本中文詳解
圖形組織圖 (G.O.) 的英文閱讀書！

Intermediate Reading

英文閱讀G.O., G.O., G.O.!

應惠蕙　編著
Peter John Wilds　審訂

Graphic Organizers for Effective Reading!

★ 精選18種實用圖形組織圖，最常用的G.O.通通有！

★ 全書共12課，多元文體搭配12種圖形組織圖，閱讀素材通通有！

★ 每課搭配G.O.練習題與4題閱讀測驗，組織架構、閱讀練習通通有！

★ 閱讀測驗加入最新大考題型——圖片題，準備大考通通有！

★ 隨書附贈翻譯與解析本，中譯詳解通通有！

★ 學校團訂贈送6回隨堂評量卷，單字測驗、翻譯練習通通有！

★ 隨書附贈朗讀音檔，雲端下載，隨載隨聽！

掌握大考新趨勢，
　搶先練習新題型！

Intermediate Reading

英文閱讀High Five

王隆興　編著

★ 全書分為5大主題：生態物種、人文歷史、科學科技、環
　境保育、醫學保健，共50篇由外籍作者精心編寫之文章。

★ 題目仿111學年度學測參考試卷命題方向設計，為未來大
　考提前作準備，搶先練習第二部分新題型——混合題。

★ 隨書附贈解析夾冊，方便練習後閱讀文章中譯及試題解
　析，並於解析補充每回文章精選的15個字彙。